HUNT FOR THE AUTUMN CLOWNS

HUNT
FOR THE AUTUMN
CLOWNS

M.S. Power

CHATTO & WINDUS

THE HOGARTH PRESS

LONDON

Published in 1983 by
Chatto & Windus. The Hogarth Press
40 William IV St, London WC2N 4DF

British Library Cataloguing in Publication Data

Power, M.S.
Hunt for the autumn clowns.
I. Title
823'.914[F]   PR6066.o/

ISBN 0-7011-2676-0
ISBN 0-7011-3916-1 Pbk

Printed in Great Britain by
Richard Clay, The Chaucer Press Ltd
Bungay, Suffolk

For Nina

Winter

The tragedy had been proclaimed. All through the late autumn and early winter, lengthening shadows moved their sinister shapes in from the grey thundering Atlantic and across the small island. Old, gaunt trees, crippled by persistent gales, welcomed them and wrapped them about their naked branches in the manner of mourning crones pulling their black shawls closer about their heads. Away down the narrow, shallow valley which divided the island from east to west, separated, too, the farming village in the north from the bustling fishing village in the south (causing mild frictions and jealousies between the two communities), a river flowed silently. It was sullen and swollen, as menacing as death: on frosty nights, when the stars bulged in their sockets and the dull brown water reflected their melancholy light, this river took on the appearance of a candle-lit procession winding its tortuous way through the harsh hillside farmland and yearning for the ocean into which it could bleed.

A quarter of a mile from the estuary, at a point where the river was sharply diverted to the left by deposits of slag from an abandoned quarry, a deeply rutted lane led towards an isolated stone structure of obscure origin. At first glance one could be forgiven for thinking it might be a church; despite the absence of a belfry and the addition of a modern one-storey pebble-dashed annexe on the seaward side, there was about the building a faintly Gothic air, enhanced, perhaps, by its mullioned windows. It was here that nineteen children now sat, waiting for the lesson to start.

7

Pericles Stort gazes about the high, cold classroom and decides he isn't going to mind it here all that much. The other children gaze also, but at him, for Pericles Stort has been used by incapable parents, in the absence of actual demons, to terrify their wayward offspring into a satisfactory state of submission. Pericles Stort will come in the dead of night and gobble you up, they warn; and, although he is barely sixteen and seems peaceful enough most of the time, his aloofness and almost total silence have made it simple to endow him with cannibalistic preferences. Yet he is a boy of quite remarkable physical beauty: lean and strong, his hair a deep rich reddish gold, his eyes dark green and bright, his mouth wide and firm and generous. It was as though his creator, perhaps distracted for a moment by problems of his own, perhaps just careless, had made some monstrous blunder and lumbered the boy with someone else's mind.

The new teacher, Miss Tricia Hudson, although she would certainly have denied it, has nonetheless been infected by the children's wariness when dealing with this strange boy. Now, she waits for him to say something. Pericles senses this and makes her wait. Finally

'Well, Pericles,' Miss Hudson ventures.

. . . but all is not well between us, she wrote to some long-forgotten friend, and we have decided to call it off . . . She found the expression particularly baleful even as she wrote it. Call it off, as one did hounds, perhaps, or yet more sinister snarling beings: ghosts which rattled dice in one's brain to determine which new torment to invoke. All of which bordered on the ridiculous, for her desire to be married had always been somewhat spurious: she suffered in some grotesque and morbid sense from an enslavement to morality which she understood to be hopeless and outdated. Nor, in fact, had there been anything to 'call off': her engagement, which her friends had in any case regarded as suspiciously nebulous, had been nothing more than an artless if understandable ruse to justify her ever

8

more visible predicament. Indeed, it was only in the final few weeks of her pregnancy that she abandoned her pretence and admitted, sometimes angrily, that her child had, from the outset, been destined to be a bastard. Her father, ecstatic for obscure reasons of his own, had in fact accepted the arrival of another Hudson as a highly propitious miracle, a miracle into which the intervention of a husband or father would have been an intrusion of appalling impertinence.

Pericles eyes her silently but encourages her with a friendly patient nod.

'Well, Pericles. And where . . . where are we going to sit, then?' The boy continues to watch her, smiling. 'Here in the front? Or would you prefer – '

'Thank you, ma'am,' says Pericles politely, and saunters to the furthermost desk in the classroom, and squats in majestic isolation.

'Oh . . . I see. Well, that's fine, Pericles. You'll like it here in school,' Miss Hudson insists, determined to win over this strange and unsettling child. 'Really you will.'

'That's nice. Thank you, ma'am,' says Pericles doubtfully.

'And you'll learn many wonderful things here,' Miss Hudson promises him, mildly alarmed at the sudden feeling that her destiny is somehow linked to this child, her own youth and this boy's in some disquieting fashion transposed. It is as though some not too antagonistic being has, after years of failure, finally succeeded in bringing the two of them together to co-operate in achieving some not yet identifiable form of mutual salvation. And she will certainly not be the cause of yet another failure. Lonely, yes, desolate as a dispossessed orphan but not a failure. She will succeed, she insists to herself although always running, afraid to risk any entanglement (for whose warmth she so desperately craves), running and being pursued through pale days and cosmetic nights – 'A Question of Frigidity' sprang at her from the glossy pages of some trivial magazine, or 'Sexual Abnormality', or, worst of all, 'The

Narcissistic Element in Post-Natal Sexual Frustration and Vaginal Paralysis' – by a terrifying darkness that persists in her mind: everyone, save herself, no matter how bitterly she labels it (hypocritical, arrogant, nay downright submissive) is accosting God and finding some faith, some hope, some *reason*.

'Yes, ma'am,' agrees Pericles.

'I'm going to do my very best to see that you all *enjoy* school,' Miss Hudson continues. 'After all, learning should be enjoyable, shouldn't it?' Some of the children seem to agree. 'I'll tell you a secret – I hated school. I thought the teachers were *awful* – '

'Yes, Miss,' chorus most of the children with some conviction.

'– ha – well, I'm going to make quite sure that things are different for you.'

'Yes, ma'am,' says Pericles suddenly.

'Thank you, Pericles. I'm glad you agree with me – '

'Yes, ma'am,' says Pericles again.

'I can see we're going to get on famously. You mustn't be afraid of me, you know. Any of you. Some children are – afraid of their teacher, I mean. I wouldn't like that at all. I'm not really an ogre, am I?' she asks, smiling nicely.

Pericles seems uninterested in the question: he sits quite still, his satchel clutched under his arm where it has been since he arrived, a sober knowing look biting the corners of his eyes. He will probably sit like this for a long while, watching the winter sun fold in through the window on cushions of chalk-dust: it looks so much like the reflection of pipe smoke thrown on a wall by a yellow light he has seen somewhere. For the moment he is alone in the classroom, unaware of the other children who scribble busily in their copybooks, bent double, sniffling, dampening the pages in front of them with twin jets of steam from their runny nostrils.

The wooden desks slope in haphazard ranks like drunken soldiers on parade and are stained and scarred by time and dirt and juvenile hieroglyphics. Here and there some forlorn misplaced child has allowed his soul to bleed from the tip of a penknife, mating calls as clear as stags' abound, hearts martyred in the name of love by arrows and, in some cases, by weapons conceived as arrows but shyly broadened and rounded and elongated to an impossible length. Most of the desks still have inkwells inserted, but for years these have been used merely as fonts for the unceremonious baptism of bluebottles, already wingless. There is a round, white-faced clock on the wall, its hour hand crippled so that only by a forty-minute deduction can one arrive at an approximate time. And it is this clock which now thumps its way through the boy's head as he swings his left leg like a pendulum. He is not listening to the teacher nor, for that matter, to the clock: he is having what everyone refers to as 'one of his fits'. It might, of course, be over soon, or it might last all day. It might never have started at all. Not that it really matters.

You know I always thought fits were dangerous, frightening things, Mam said to Vigy. You know like with that thing dogs get.

Aren't they? Vigy wanted to know.

Well, his don't seem to be.

Not yet.

I don't think there's that much wrong with the boy, Mam said loyally.

Oh, come on now, Mam –

He just likes to daydream, if you ask me.

Dad doesn't think so.

Oh, I know your father thinks he's mad. But he thinks everyone's –

You must admit he's odd.

Maybe it's his being by himself so much – would you think?

Maybe, Mam.

But then he *likes* to be off and away by himself, doesn't he?

Hmm.

I suppose school will do him some good but it *does* seem a bit late in the day for that.

No harm sending him, Vigy said.

I suppose not.

Get him out from under Dad's feet anyway, and that can't be bad for any of us.

That's true, Vigy. Very true. Oh, I do hope everything works out all right. I get this awful feeling sometimes –

Don't be silly, Mam. Of course everything will be all right.

Oh, I hope so.

Well, Pericles, said the new teacher Miss Hudson.

Yes, ma'am, said Pericles politely.

I'm not an ogre.

No, ma'am.

You mustn't be afraid of me.

Thank you, ma'am. She had a nice music to her voice and she smelled of the same babysoap that Mam used to use on him when she washed him in the big metal tub in front of the fire on Saturday nights.

Eventually: it is now time to take your satchel from under your arm and place it on the desk beside you, carefully. Pericles takes the satchel from under his arm and places it on the desk beside him, carefully. It had belonged to his brother, as had most of his clothes, but it is still in good condition and the new stitching along the side (put in with great skill by Uncle Peter) has been dirtied down nicely so it doesn't show, and the buckles gleam because Pericles shines them every evening. He is very fond of his satchel.

Waste not, want not, Mam said philosophically as she dusted off the satchel with the palm of her hand and admired Uncle Peter's handiwork. He did it so neatly, didn't he, Pericles? she asked. Ah, he was always so clever with his hands, she sighed. He could mend anything. Simply anything, anything at all. And if he couldn't nobody could.

Want not. She wrapped a sandwich of cold bacon in a piece

of coloured paper and tucked it away in the satchel, buckling it down safely. Waste not. The paper had once enclosed a flamboyant headscarf (purple silk across which surrealistic gnus pranced) sent by her sister at Christmas, and had been folded carefully and put away in a drawer of the kitchen dresser for future use. Her sister (always referred to as 'poor' Auntie Girlie) had arrived every Christmas morning at the farm with some small gift for each member of the family until, out of the blue and at the advanced age of sixty-three, she had astounded them all by marrying the blacksmith, some thirty years her junior. He had packed her bags and bustled her off to Canada, and she was never heard of again. Not, that is, until she died and then a parcel arrived stuffed with gifts for all the family which, it transpired, she had wrapped to celebrate some Christmas long since passed and forgotten or not bothered to send: a silk tie and a china borzoi, a fur-lined leather helmet with the label still attached to prove it had cost seven dollars and been made in Newfoundland, a pair of strong, thick-soled boots for Big Mike, two frilly, low-cut blouses, a small collection of strange gadgets for the kitchen which were doomed never to be fathomed or used, and a hunting knife for Pericles. So, and it had seemed much better this way, they had opened their Christmas presents in mid-summer and thanked the donor as each gift was unwrapped. It was easier to thank her now she was dead; anyone who sent such marvellous gifts was certainly in heaven, and heaven was a great deal closer to them than Canada.

Well, Pericles, said the new teacher, Miss Hudson, smiling and smelling of babysoap on a weekday.

Yes, ma'am, said Pericles.

And where shall we sit.

Pericles opens the satchel that has been so nicely stitched by Uncle Peter.

It's nothing but a bloody waste of time and energy sending that damn moron to school, Dad muttered sourly and repeated: a bloody waste of time.

Father Redmond said he should go, Mam insisted, hoping clerical intervention would prove decisive.

How would he know? Dad demanded. He's about as mad as the boy himself.

Don't talk about the priest like that, Mam said but quietly as though she sensed her husband had come uncomfortably near the truth. Father Redmond's a good man, she added.

Aye, good and mad if you ask me, Dad told her firmly, a tiny grin, prematurely born, fighting for life on his lips.

Anyway, school can't do him any harm, Mam insisted hopefully. Run along, Pericles.

Huh, said Dad.

'Bye, Mam, said Pericles.

'Bye, dear.

Pericles fingers the coloured packet in the satchel for a while and then transfers his attention to the hunting knife stuck in the top of one of the strong, thick-soled boots which Big Mike had given him when they lost their shape. He thinks about putting the knife in his satchel but is distracted by the clock on the wall which ticks rhythmically in his brain. There is a name etched in ornate script on the enamel dial: *Joseph Butterworth Fecit*. He tries to read this but abandons the exercise when the clock starts to skip alternate beats. Suddenly the clock musters a forlorn effort and attempts to strike but the cotton-wool stuffed between the chimes suffocates the tones and it simply whirs like a thrush fluffing its feathers.

Run along, Pericles.

'Bye, Mam.

'Bye, dear.

One of the twins clung to his leg and mouthed don't go, dribbling.

Pericles begins to scratch his crotch, opening his legs and watching his actions carefully.

The best place for Pericles would be in school, Father

Redmond assured Mam and Dad. It will do him the world of good to mix with other children. I can certainly think of no better place. And under the circumstances, Denis, we think it would be the best place for you until such time as you have overcome this, eh, problem, his friend the Bishop said. We shall pray for you, of course.

Of course. But good God – Father Redmond stood perfectly still staring at the prelate while the enormity of the insult and disillusionment washed over his soul. As if – and who else but a friend would dare suggest it – as if he had any problem apart, of course, from an interfering hierarchy. But nevertheless he recognised an elusive charity in the rebuke. For even as the words of banishment (as he somewhat melodramatically liked to consider them), even as they rattled in his brain like wooden cartwheels on a cobbled road, even then he knew he was not quite sober. Although he could have been, he assured himself, but perhaps not at that particular moment, standing there in inconceivable anguish but coping, bravely and quite admirably, with a monstrous hangover thunderclapping around his skull. But what right had the Lord Bishop to assume that this presumably temporary lapse was indeed a problem, or that it would be a lesser problem or, perish the thought, no problem at all at some unspecified date in the future? And again: what right had this empurpled figure of some dignity, while he himself had spent eternities on his knees suffering the tortures of every martyr in some spiritual madhouse on behalf of God the Father, Son and Holy Ghost for hours on end and displaying a magnificent rectitude on behalf of his uninterested congregation without even the assistance of a decent drink, from what conceivable standpoint of justice or charity did the Bishop imagine he could judge what was the problem? It was the letter, of course: that mad accursed letter which the Bishop now held in his hand and waved from time to time as though to underline the wisdom of his decision. If only he could remember why he had sent it and what, indeed, he had written in it!

– simply must try, the bishop's gentle voice penetrated.
– ?

I don't mind telling you, Denis, there has been considerable pressure on me to suspend you.

Ah, I'm quite used to that –

Used to – ?

Suspension. Upside down by my toenails while the whole world spins around me. Not a pretty sight, I might add.

For goodness sake do stop feeling so inanely sorry for yourself. You simply refuse, don't you, to try and understand the precariousness of your position.

Oh, but I do, Matthew. But not, I think, in the way you mean. No more than you can understand – never mind.

If only you would put your trust in God and try –

Indeed, said Father Redmond, nodding solemnly, although he already knew he could find no God in which to trust, knew he had little attention, little capability for the further effort of trying.

Pericles opens one end of the coloured package, careful not to tear the paper. Get help, I can't swim, a voice screams in his ear, so close that he jerks his head about violently. Get help, damn you, boy. Then he went under again. Pericles was astounded that his Grandfather could not swim. He simply could not believe it, so he stood silently on the river bank and watched intently just to make sure. The old man split the water again, bobbing up like a monstrous cork, blue in the face and very frightened.

Now don't you eat your sandwich until you see the other children eating theirs, Mam warned him kindly and patted his head.

No, Mam.

Good boy.

Good for nothing, Dad said.

Hush, Mam told him.

Then Grandad went under again, trying desperately to

scream. Pericles was forced to believe the old man's incapability now and hated him for drowning; and when he watched the bloated body being hauled from the river three days later he detested his Grandfather even more for allowing himself to become so disfigured.

Hey Pe-e-ericles, yelled Poppy Burn.

Hello, Poppy.

Hey, Pericles, whispered Poppy, can yours swell up too?

– ?

I bet yours is more interesting though, eh?

Don't know, Pericles confessed. And bigger too, he heard Poppy say. Maybe.

I bet it is.

Pericles fumbles with his crotch, getting worried, trying as hard as he can to remember what Mam told him to do.

If you want to go out, Mam explained patiently, raise your hand and the teacher will let you. She'll tell you where it is. Do you understand that?

Yes, Mam.

Damn fool, Dad muttered.

Right now Pericles wants to go badly but he has forgotten Mam's admonition. Instead he gets up quietly and shambles out of the classroom.

And don't drop your pants, roared Big Mike who knew everything. Just open your fly, he added and guffawed.

Leave the boy alone, Mam scolded. I haven't forgotten that you still wetted the bed at his age.

Big Mike blushed crimson and went out slamming the kitchen door. Mam chuckled. But you better do as he said, she told Pericles. Open your buttons and close them again when you're finished.

Yes, Mam.

Good boy.

Pericles concentrates on opening his buttons but by the time he has them all undone he has already wet himself. Immediately he closes them again, carefully, and returns to the class-room where the teacher smells sweetly of babysoap. The clock still has strange writing imprinted on its dial but it has stopped functioning in his brain. Miss Hudson, who has been busily writing on the blackboard, steps back to inspect her work. Pericles inspects it also: the different coloured chalks she has used look very pretty. Something, though has been moved: watery November sun now cuts through the tall windows at a different angle, spotlighting his satchel and the nicely wrapped package on top of it. Pericles likes the way the coloured paper shines in the sun, its shadow making a second, even larger package beside it. He is getting on famously.

The teacher is drawing on the blackboard again, still using the pretty coloured chalks: a pink figure with straight un-bending limbs like a matchstick child is balanced on a sort of trestle surrounded by green and blue and red matchstick adults. THE BABE IN THE – he is able to make out, laboriously mouthing each word to himself. There is one more word but this means nothing to him.

' – and this is the Virgin Mary,' Miss Hudson announces, indicating, in a mildly triumphant way, an adoring blue shape with short straight yellow parallel lines radiating from its head.

We really should get you out into the sun, you know, Miss Hudson, the matron said.

A little later, perhaps.

Tricia Hudson sat very upright and rigid on the straight-backed, cane-seated chair facing the open window across which, in the afternoon 'rest' period, white net curtains would be drawn but which now billowed gently on either side of the window like the skirts of imaginary angels. Perhaps it was just her body that had been sundered, she mused, slowly emerging from the protection of sedatives into an astonished detach-ment, while her spirit renewed itself endlessly; unless it, too, had acquired an addiction to decay.

Why not let me fix a seat for you on the veranda, the

matron's voice persisted kindly enough but with that brittle edge so often adopted by those who are convinced they know what is best for others and who take unkindly to being disobeyed. I'll wrap a nice warm rug over your knees and you'll be grand and warm and comfy.

No. Honestly. Thank you. Tomorrow, perhaps. I just don't feel up to any sunshine right now.

Tut-tut. Well, we must get some colour back in those pretty cheeks. We can't have you going home looking all pale and peaky, can we?

Tomorrow.

We might not have the sun with us tomorrow, dear. You know how temperamental the weather is. Just for half an hour – to please me?

Please, matron. Not now. I would much sooner just sit here where I am for today.

Very well, if you insist.

I do, said Tricia Hudson her face tightening into those unaccustomed stubborn lines it had only once before assumed: when she had instructed them to take her child away for adoption. For eight months she had thrived perversely on the anguish of that sacrifice, and on the discomfort she inflicted on anyone who came in contact with her, until the nightly visits from a randy adulterous spectre named Jonathan resembling (as far as she would allow herself to recall) the elusive father of her child had driven her screaming to the sanatorium. And it had taken the best part of another full year for the lecherous nightwatchman to be castrated, but he could be remembered now as a not ungentle creature with a rather weak chin, who had just returned from a ten-month stint sheep-farming in New Zealand and in that short time managed to affect the nasal Kiwi twang almost to perfection, who played rugby, liked Pushkin and Goya and Charlie Byrd, and wore American-style underpants.

'The Virgin Mary, mother of baby Jesus,' Miss Hudson tells

19

the class crisply.

Listen to me, boy, Dad warned ominously. You keep well clear of that Poppy Burn.

Bill! Mam exclaimed.

Better to warn the fool, Dad told her civilly.

He's not that sort of boy, Mam said.

Doesn't have to be. That Poppy would lie down under a bloody ginnet.

Two, said Big Mike significantly.

That's enough of that talk, Big Mike, Mam snapped.

You can keep out of this, Dad told him.

It's *him* you're trying to keep out, retorted Big Mike grinning, determined not to be put down.

Pericles looks down at his crotch. And bigger, too, I bet, Poppy Burn surmised hopefully.

'Now then – does everyone understand what I have drawn on the blackboard?' Miss Hudson would like to know.

'Yes, Miss,' the children sing out.

Pericles says nothing.

'Good. Are there any questions at all?'

'No, Miss.'

'In that case I would like someone to help me to – '

Get help, damn you, boy, Grandad screamed. His bloated body with coarse grey hairs covering its chest and shoulders and back looked like little more than a gigantic mess of eel-bait. Pericles wanted to puncture the obscene hulk the first time he saw it laid out on the table in the parlour, puncture it and bring it back to its normal uninflated size, back to life, perhaps, and get some good reason for its refusal to swim.

Jesus! What's that bloody moron up to with that damn hunting knife? Dad shouted, sounding scared.

Pericles quickly hid his knife by sliding it down the top of his thick soled boot.

'Pericles – what *are* you doing?' the teacher demands out of the blue.

The boy stares at her confused, his brain suddenly out of rhythm.

'What are you playing with?'

'Nothing, ma'am.'

All the other children in the classroom turn their heads and eye him suspiciously, giggling covertly. Pericles frowns. Somewhere this has already happened to him. Or something like it.

What's that bloody moron up to with that damned hunting knife, Dad shouted, and all his brothers and sisters turned and stared at him, openly smirking since familiarity had blunted their fear and made Pericles seem tame enough.

Pericles folds the open end of his package, carefully following the creases his mother has made in the paper.

Please don't tear the paper, Mam pleaded. It's so pretty and we can use it again, can't we? See, she added philosophically, if I hadn't saved it in the first place we would have had to wrap your sandwich in plain brown paper and that wouldn't have been nearly as nice, would it?

No, Mam.

Well then.

'Are you all right, Pericles?'

'Yes, ma'am.'

'You're quite sure?'

'Yes, ma'am.'

'You're not ill?'

Pericles thinks about this. 'No, ma'am,' he says finally.

'Well, then, if you want to leave the room again I hope you'll ask my permission. Where would I be if I allowed everyone to wander in and out willy-nilly?' asked Miss Hudson sternly, immediately regretting her severity and adding a hint of mirth to her voice. 'You *will* ask, won't you?'

'Yes, ma'am.'

'Good.'

'I'm sorry, ma'am.'

'That's all right, Pericles.'

'Thank you, ma'am.'

'Good.'

Hardly, the elderly doctor told Tricia, pausing to remove his spectacles and rub them vigorously with a dotted silk handkerchief he produced from his inside pocket with a magician's flourish, but then it's not all bad either, is it? Heh, nothing ever is, really. Anyhow, there's precious little more we can do for you. It's simply a question of your learning to cope with everyday life again. And that shouldn't be too terribly difficult. You're a highly intelligent young lady, and a very pretty one too, I might add. And that, according to the criteria by which one observed such things, Tricia Hudson knew to be true. It had been true of her then at twenty and was equally true of her now sixteen years later that she gave an irresistible impression of someone about to be beautiful. It was as though fate had generously overlooked her trauma, overlooked, too, any personal neglect or even any payment due to the years, and fixed her age at some unidentifiable moment of great happiness in the past.

And from the past, perhaps from that very precious moment of happiness, through the rows of school desks, Tricia's father made his way towards her, responding generously to the inquisitive glance of each child, patting one or two on the head and enquiring after their health, her father whose reckless and peculiarly abstract habits still smacked of mild and good-natured insanity. The tiny pen-and-ink sketch she carried in a gold heart-shaped locket about her neck depicted him as a middle-aged sartorial gentleman sucking a chin-warming Meerschaum (something she was certain he had never done, considering as he did tobacco smoke to be that 'narcotic cloud which veiled the sight of sense from the sight of imagery', whatever he meant by that), with twinkling eyes beneath a floppy fedora, a ridiculously beaked nose which seemed to rely on the small Hitlerian moustache beneath it for its balance, and a strong pointed chin which had, at various times, been

22

adorned by beards of various design; her father, with his suicidal addiction to gambling, who set out so confidently each morning armed with the borrowed wisdom of the racing tipsters to make his fortune. Sadly he had always failed. Berated by his wife and scorned by his many friends he took to locking himself away in the potting shed, perhaps consulting the geraniums, and devising elaborate systems in increasingly frantic efforts to beat the bookmakers. None of these systems, ingenious though they may have been, ever worked out the way they were expected to. He had once promulgated the theory that substantial sums could be won by wagering only on such animals as were racing under their particular birth sign and he was grossly affronted when they failed to oblige.

The coloured chalk screams relentlessly on the blackboard and Pericles winces.

No, Bill. Not now. Not again.

Why can't Dad leave her alone, Vigy wanted to know. You'd think he'd be dried up at his age.

Hell no, said Big Mike who knew everything.

But Dad's hurting her, Vigy insisted.

That's the way they like it, said Big Mike confidently. You should know that.

Why should *I* know?' Vigy bridled.

You're as easy to lay as Poppy Burn.

I am not.

I hear you are.

I am not.

They say if you want to learn how to do it go to Vigy Stort, Big Mike goaded happily.

Bugger what *they* say, Vigy snorted scornfully.

You better just hope they don't start saying it where Dad can hear, Big Mike warned. He'd bloody crucify you.

He'd have to catch me first.

Catch you? Christ, that's not hard. Bet you could even teach me a thing or two.

You're too thick to learn *anything*.

Oh yeah?

Yeah.

You'll learn all sorts of nice things at school, Mam told him.

You'll learn many wonderful things here at school, Miss Hudson told him.

'Bye, Mam. Yes, ma'am.

Pericles stared at the clothes laid out on the old wooden blanket chest at the foot of the bed he had shared with Big Mike since he was twelve. Only the shirt was new: the corduroy trousers and the tweed jacket with the leather patches on the elbows and leather strips on the cuffs had been Young Bill's before he emigrated to Sydney and got himself killed. Just two weeks into a grand new life for himself and he gets himself bitten in two by a shark, Grandad enjoyed telling the men in the pub. Can you credit a thing like that? Fine job handed to him on a plate and young Tessa Finn huffing and puffing to go and join him and the stupid bugger has to go and get in the road of a bloody foreign shark. God, some people have *no* sense, do they?

Pericles stroked the blue-and grey-striped shirt, brushing the flannel in one direction like he would the cat.

Pss pss and the wary shy animal slipped closer to him, belly to the ground. It lay at his feet, its feverish yellow eyes staring at him. Pericles took the chicken bones from his pocket and offered them, but the animal backed off, glancing rapidly in every direction. The boy was undismayed. He understood mistrust. He placed the bones in a small neat pile on the ground and retreated a few paces: with sharp crackles like burning kindlewood the food was devoured. The animal knew there would be no more that evening and moved off, choosing its cover, melting into the dusk. Pericles stared longingly at the vacant space where the creature had been and wished he could vanish just like that. Maybe he would, one day. And he thought seriously about this in his own laboured way as he crossed the field to the farmhouse.

Haw, haw, haw, haw, there! Grandad was delighted as he handed over the bloody axe to Big Mike for cleaning. Got the thievin' bastard, he roared and flung the decapitated fox on the woodpile beside the kitchen stove and went off coughing and chuckling to himself to get a knife. Pericles, where's that grand sharp knife of yours?

Pericles said nothing. The blood dripped from one log to the next, and with each drip the mutilated little creature seemed to shrink a fraction more. In his mind's eye Pericles could already see his frightened companion being skinned, its pelt stretched out on cruciform stakes to dry, its flesh tossed indifferently to the dog and cats. He felt a small chop bone in his pocket and wondered what he would do with it now.

Boy, I'm talking to you. Where's that knife you got from your poor Auntie Girlie?

Pericles eyed his Grandfather sullenly.

Leave him be, Mam advised. I think he's having one of his fits.

So what?

They're like sleepwalking –

Sleepwalking?

Yes. The doctor told me that, Mam lied and hoped Grandad would believe her. You shouldn't wake him up suddenly, she explained.

Bloody rubbish.

You don't know better than the doctors, Grandad, Mam insisted.

Doctors! Grandad scoffed. Bad as priests they are.

You can use the kitchen knife, Mam told him. It's nice and sharp.

Call that sharp? Grandad demanded, running his tough, earth-encrusted thumb down the blade. It wouldn't cut butter.

It's quite sharp enough for what you want.

Damn that boy.

You leave Pericles alone, Grandad. He's not well.

Nothing wrong with him that a good kick on the backside wouldn't cure.

Pericles patted his new shirt again before he got into bed. Perhaps he thought it might leave him during the night if he did not show it some small kindness.

Get plenty of sleep tonight, Mam advised him kindly. You've got all that learning to cope with tomorrow, don't forget.

Yes, Mam.

That's my good boy.

Learning! Big Mike snorted. That one?

Don't always pick on him, Big Mike. You weren't all that bright when you were at school if you remember. You never did learn how to write properly.

I managed all right, muttered Big Mike.

So will Pericles. Won't you, Pericles?

Yes, Mam.

Of course you will. Turn out better than all of them put together I shouldn't wonder.

Yes, Mam.

And then you'll get a wonderful job and look after your mother when she gets old, won't you, Mam fantasized.

Yes, Mam. I will.

You're the only one who loves his mother, Pericles. If anything happened to you I don't know what would become of me.

Nothing'll happen to me, Mam.

Oh, I hope not.

Nothing'll happen to you, Mam.

Thank you, Pericles, Mam said gently, a little puzzled, and kissed him on the cheek. Off you go to bed now. And sweet dreams.

Thank you, Mam. 'Night.

'Night, son. God bless.

'This is the nativity scene,' says Miss Hudson, somehow managing to incorporate a genuflection in her voice. 'The

26

birthday of our Saviour Jesus.' You should have thought of that before you . . . her mother's nagging voice trailed off in a haze of shamed and pinched rebuke. It was most surprising really, not only had she, Tricia Hudson, not been alarmed, she had been devoid of any air of remorse whatsoever. True, she had presented a somewhat haggard face to the world as she manoeuvered her bulging abdomen around obstacles which had never before impeded her progress, but as for caring . . . not until much later, when the day-old child had been taken away from her, had her own persistent, objective self, perhaps exhausted by sitting apart and watching her turbulent nightmares, at last gathered up its weariness and withdrawn from her altogether. It had occurred to her that she might, ultimately, be in the grip of something against which her inadequate defences could avail her little. But she had not the slightest intention of giving in just then. On the contrary she intended to brazen things out (as her mother, with her characteristic vulgar prudishness, had put it), carrying with her, although more like some defiant hump on her back than the more familiar and spiritually convenient cross, the cheap remarks and bawdy winks. Indeed, on the face of it, up to and including the dreadful moments of her child's delivery (while she abandoned all hope of her own deliverance, abandoned, too, even the slimmest prospect of some modest pact with God) she had certainly succeeded in pulling herself together.

Every day's a birthday at Stort's place, Pericles heard one of the workmen say as they leaned on their spades, resting.

Aye, more power to his elbow.

What's his elbow got to do with it, you stupid bugger?

That's where he gets his grease from. Haw, haw.

Bugger all grease he needs at this stage.

Haw.

More like oakum he'd be wanting!

Then they spotted Pericles watching them and looked away quickly.

Thump. Thump.

That's the way they like it, said Big Mike.

Fat lot you'd know, said Vigy.

But what's Dad doing, Pericles asked, curious.

Never mind, said Big Mike.

Tell him, whispered Vigy. It's high time he knew what's happening.

I'm not going to tell him, Big Mike whispered back.

Because you don't know, said Vigy mockingly.

Like hell I don't.

Well, tell the poor sod, then. He has to know sometime and it may as well be now.

Aw, all right . . .

We're waiting, giggled Vigy.

Well, Big Mike explained to Pericles, you know what you saw that bull of Gallagher's doing the other day?

What was that? Pericles asked, not remembering the incident.

Jesus.

Vigy roared with laughter from her bed in the corner. She was the only one in the family who had a bed to herself and was very proud of the fact.

What's so bloody funny, Big Mike demanded.

You and Gallagher's bull, you great ape.

I'm only trying to make it so he'll understand.

Understand? Jesus – God help any girl he tries to mount the way Gallagher's bull does.

Aw, shut your mouth, said Big Mike.

Why can't you tell him straight?

I was giving him an example so he could picture –

But Mam doesn't take it a bit like that, stupid. God, no wonder all the girls in the factory are laughing about you!

I know bloody well she doesn't. You shut your mouth or I'll soon ram something home in you and we'll see who's laughing.

Oh yeah, said Vigy derisively. You and who else to show you

the right way? But she stopped teasing him. Maybe, she thought, she would let him try it some time. Besides laughing all the girls said he did it really well, better than anyone any of them had ever had.

'And next month it will be Christmas time,' Miss Hudson announces happily as though in some way she was personally responsible, or at least had a hand in it.

Pericles looks up at the clock: Joseph Butterworth indicates almost eleven and the thrush would soon be trying to free itself once again.

They like foxes better than rabbits, Grandad announced dogmatically as the ravenous old farm dog ripped the tiny shrivelled carcass to pieces, snapping indiscriminately at the cats each time they tried to share the spoils. Suddenly it jerked its head upwards to swallow a large chunk and a glob of congealed blood shot away and hit Pericles in the mouth. For a moment he was too terrified to move, then he bent double and vomited, the sickness tearing out of his bowels like broken glass.

Haw, what's the matter with you, boy? Never seen a dead fox before? Grandad's dull little eyes sparkled momentarily.

Don't be at him, Mam snapped. Can't you see he's sick. Come with me, Pericles, and I'll get you a drink of water.

God, woman, the way you molly that child! Grandad said shaking his head. He'll never be able to stand on his own two feet.

He's right, you know, Dad put in. You're always taking the boy's side against us. Treat him like a girl you do, sometimes.

Don't you pay any heed to them, Pericles, Mam whispered. You're my little boy, aren't you? Come now and we'll get you that drink of nice cold water.

The thrush fluffs its feathers, its tiny heart thumping eleven times urgently.

'This is Saint Joseph. And these – these five men here – well, who do you think they are?' Miss Hudson asks.

29

'Shepherds, Miss.'

'Good boy, Douglas. That's quite right. Shepherds. And here looking at her new-born baby is Mary,' Miss Hudson is saying, smelling of babysoap.

Do be good at school, won't you? Mam pleaded, worried.

I still say it's a damn fool waste of time and energy, Dad insisted but sounding resigned.

I know you still say that, Bill. You've said it twenty times at least. But Father Redmond said he should go and that's that, Mam insisted firmly.

Damned interfering priest, Dad muttered.

But Mam heard him and Bill! she said, shocked.

Priests! Dad said and left the kitchen.

It had been the scene in the confessional, of course, which had been the penultimate catastrophe in his descent to disgrace. His price for forgiving the penitent so readily was to have them draw inexorably closer while he, aware of his stupor and of the enormity of his dereliction, tried with as much dignity as he could command to dissuade them from intruding, as he thought of it, on his degradation and sorrow. Absurdly, he wanted to be alone in his little confession box, while with bewildering rapidity the latticed wooden shutters crashed open, as did the hearts and souls of people who obviously knew nothing about sin. Father Redmond felt like some poor idiot trying to bring light to the world with only a shredded fragment of flex between himself and eternal damnation. In his state of rarefied obliqueness he was aware that death and damnation frightened him not at all, aware that he feared nothing at that moment which might tend to sober him up. There above him as he lay on his back outside the confessional (lay on his back outside the confessional? Lay on his back outside the confessional!) were poised the sins of the world, stretching out and down to him, supplicating, pleading to be cleansed. He did not like being prostrate on his back, he did not like it at all. It was far from funny, it was doubtless yet another example of man's unnecessary suffering; and it could hardly be considered a dignified posture for a man of the cloth. Still, he consoled himself, perhaps it was symbolic, the symbolism for the moment eluding him. Holy sweet and generous God! All at once, terribly, he was crying. Everything was being torn from him. Oh, God, said Father Redmond, oh, dear, dear, God. He felt himself thrashing about, wildly trying to stand upright. He was conscious of people laughing at him but, what was infinitely more unreal, these same people were trying to help him. The very souls who came to him for solace and understanding now held out their hands to him, offering him understanding and solace (and maybe even forgiveness although this, he realized, was unlikely), helping him to his feet; then, hurt by his embarrassment, scurrying away without waiting for his thanks.

Pericles stares at the blackboard on which Miss Hudson has most artistically enlarged the scene since he last looked at it. Now it is crowded with coloured shapes: two-legged, four-legged, kneeling, sitting, standing, all clustered about the mysterious pink figure on the trestle. Pericles signals the teacher by standing up, but Miss Hudson, engrossed in her multi-coloured miracle, does not see him, so he walks between the rows of desks towards her. He walks with exaggerated stealth and care so as not to upset the teacher by making noise. He stops behind her, waiting.

Don't you ever creep up on me like that again, Pericles Stort, Poppy Burn shouted at him.

– ?

You frightened the living daylights out of me.

Sorry, Poppy.

Sorry. Huh.

Pericles hung his head, smiling to himself, and shuffled a little dance.

What you want, anyway? Poppy wanted to know.

Nothing.

What you mean nothing? What did you come sneaking up on me for if you wanted nothing?

Pericles started to get confused.

Oh, never mind. Here, let me feel you, Poppy said in her dull, matter-of-fact voice.

Pericles stepped back alarmed.

Christ, I only want to *feel* you, for God's sake. That's all. Pericles relaxed a little.

Anyone would think I was going to eat you. Haven't you ever done this before? Pericles shook his head. Damn well time you did, then. Here. Take it out.

Pericles felt the excitement stirring between his legs as Poppy Burn fondled him. He pressed himself closer to the girl and squeezed her bottom, like a double mandolin, between his hands.

Hmm, Poppy moaned, closing her eyes and rocking the two of them back and forth slowly. She undulated her hips and sighed deeply. Hmmm, she groaned as Pericles tuned her mandolin and played it gently. Hoy, she grunted suddenly and stepped back. Not there, she said petulantly. Your goddam stupid finger doesn't go there, you daft idiot.

Oh –

Christ! Do I have to teach all you lot everything.

Sorry, Poppy.

You're always sorry.

Pericles watches Miss Hudson's bottom carefully. Fatter and rounder. But quite playable nonetheless. He takes one step closer, unaware of the uncanny stillness that has descended on the classroom as the other children watch him intently, hardly daring, it seems, to breathe, small lights of anticipation and terror flickering brightly in their eyes.

Miss Hudson is systematically covering the upper regions of the blackboard with yellow dots. Toc. Toc. Toc, Stars and planets appear, imaginary firmaments of her galactic imagination glow chalkily. Toc. Toc. Each cosmos comes into being in perfect rhythm to the metronomic demands of Joseph Butterworth.

I bet you're a great one for pocket billiards, suggested Poppy Burn coyly.

– ?

Playing with yourself, stupid.

No, said Pericles.

Come off it! You can't have slept with Big Mike all this time and done nothing. I know him, the dirty –

No, said Pericles again.

I don't believe it! Pericles shrugged his shoulders. Nobody ever believes him. You mean you never *once* – Jesus! You're a virgin!

Something niggled at the back of Pericles's mind. Maybe he had done what Poppy was suggesting. He had certainly had this exciting feeling before. Gradually a hazy picture began to take shape in his brain: it was summer and very hot. Mam washed him in the metal tub in the garden instead of in front of the fire. Mam's hand was soft and warm and caressing as she sudded the babysoap between his legs. She dallied over his tiny penis – his little pickle she christened it . . .

Miss Hudson's buttocks strain as the moon is consigned to the top left-hand corner of the blackboard.

You know what it's *for*, don't you? Poppy Burn wanted to know. I mean you don't still think it's just for pissing through, do you? Pericles kept a shrewd silence. You know what happens if you shove that thing *in* me?

– ?

I'll have a baby, dafty, she announced triumphantly, standing lopsided and watching him quizzically, her eyes gleaming hopefully.

Pericles was amazed.

I mean it, Poppy assured him. Put it in – and shoot, she added as an afterthought.

You keep well clear of that Poppy Burn, Dad warned him ominously.

He will, Mam said. He's a good boy. Aren't you, Pericles?

Good be damned, Dad snorted. That little slut would have his pants down before he even woke up.

Haw, roared Big Mike. Fat lot of difference that would make. Silly bugger wouldn't know what to do.

Don't talk like that, Big Mike, Mam said cautiously and was relieved that Dad backed her up: You shut your dirty mouth, Dad snapped. You weren't so bloody clever with Poppy yourself if all I hear is true. Big Mike blushed furiously and Dad roared with laughter at his son's embarrassment, and Gran cackled from beside the oven although she had no idea what was funny.

You pay no heed to them, son, Mam whispered in his ear. And she held him very close and rocked him gently, consoling her own loneliness at the same time.

Pericles wants to touch Miss Hudson's bottom: all his life he has had to feel things if only to prove to himself that they are not just skitterings of his mind. So many things seem to be. The teacher has her tongue out now, flickering her lips like an adder. She is also panting a little. Pericles stretches out his hand and touches the right mandolin, tuning.

For what, under the circumstances, seems an abnormally long time Tricia Hudson does not move: possibly transfixed by some hypnotic radiance from her own misshapen moon. She refuses categorically to believe her own senses, refuses, too, even to investigate. She waits, she knows not why, for it to happen again. But nothing happens. Almost as though the waiting had frightened her more than the act she swings round, fully intending to scream. But the boy confronting her, smiling and inoffensive, so totally at odds with the visions that had flashed across her mind, completely disarms her and her intended scream crumbles to a nervous chirp.

'What is it now, Pericles?' she asks, her voice controlled, her eyes scrupulously avoiding the excited, inquisitive class.

Pericles continues to smile, not saying anything: he has long

34

since forgotten what he wanted.

'I suggest you return to your place, Pericles. Go on. Back you go this instant.'

Obediently, but not before giving her a wistful, unsettling look, Pericles makes his way back to his seat.

'And you will kindly not leave your desk again.'

'No, ma'am.'

'If you want something simply raise your hand, do you understand that?'

'Yes, Ma'am.'

'Good. Maybe now we can get on with some work.'

They always pretend they don't want it, you know, Big Mike who knew everything said. Believe you me the more they tell you to stop the more they're hankering after it.

Bloody typical, said Vigy.

What you mean, typical? Big Mike demanded.

You men always think we're mad for you to have us.

I know you are.

You should hear what they say about you in the factory!

Like what? Big Mike wanted to know.

Like the way you're always panting about begging for a bit and only too damn grateful if you get a nibble.

Lying bitches.

They can't *all* be lying.

Huh.

The Director of the Teachers' Training College made a little speech, written for the occasion. The graduates, Tricia Hudson among them, listened, their faces flat with boredom. All you young people, he began primly, all you young teachers as you now are, have taken upon yourselves a mission comparable only to that of the holy priesthood. Into your hands will be entrusted the most sacred obligation of forming young minds in the way of righteousness. It is a task that will not be easy. Thanks will be small, trials and tribulations great. There will be times when you will find yourselves overwhelmed by doubts.

You will sometimes be frightened and lonely. Times when you may even be physically threatened . . .

Tricia Hudson wonders if she has just been physically threatened. Of course not. She recognizes that she has been expecting something like this to happen ever since she accepted the post, recognizes, also, that in some curious way she had rather enjoyed the experience. As though to repudiate this Tricia Hudson announces firmly: 'And this, this lady in blue, is the Most Holy Virgin Mary.'

Pericles smiles at her again, morally supporting her.

Don't you give that teacher any lip or I'll have the skin off your back, Dad said by way of farewell. The ancient Austin finally spluttered into life and rattled out of the yard. And don't you think for one minute that I'm driving him to school every morning, Dad warned Mam.

I know, Mam said. Just this once so he won't feel so alone, poor little mite.

Damn fool likes to be alone, Dad told her.

Well, at school he'll have to mix with other children and that might be the making of him, Mam retorted hopefully.

That's the bloody trouble, he's not a bloody child. Doesn't even try to act like one. Like some damn wild animal, he is.

Don't frighten him, Mam begged.

Frighten him! Dad exploded. Frighten *him*!

The old truck had a hard time of it on the hill that sloped from the farm up through the village to the school. The threadbare tyres finding no grip in the slush and mud. Finally, it wheezed, like Grandma first thing in the morning, and capitulated.

Goddam it to hell, Dad swore. Get out, boy, and help me push.

Pericles took off the boots which Mam had polished up nicely for him the night before and stepped out into the lane. He wore no socks, never had, but with his feet on the ground, the cold mud seeping between his toes, he felt safer and

36

happier. The air was crisp and new, not yesterday's, not yet heavy with the peat smoke that by midday would hang over the valley and seemed to need the cover of darkness to make its escape to the sea. Still, in about an hour, Pericles knew, the sun would try and warm things which was nice.

They heaved the truck to the top of the incline and rested a while, Dad blowing hard, mopping the top of his head where there should have been hair with a polka-dotted bandana from Manitoba and spitting, drawing mucus from his nose and screwing the saliva into the mud with the toe of his wellington. Pericles watched this performance in silence and tucked it away in his mind along with: Dad's trousers tucked into the top of his boots, the enormous bulge in Dad's crotch twice the size of his own but not much bigger than Big Mike's.

It's a waste of time telling you, I suppose, Dad supposed, but try and learn something at school.

Yes, Dad.

Dad stared at him. I wish I knew if anything I said got through that thick skull of yours.

Yes, Dad.

Your mother's only trying to help you, Dad told him. And I am, too.

Yes, Dad.

Pericles felt swamped by the number of children at the school: he had never been isolated among so many strangers in his life. He glanced about, furtively trying to locate a familiar face, Poppy Burn perhaps: there was one girl who looked like her, who should have been her, who probably was her, but she ignored him so she couldn't have been Poppy.

He'll make a right bloody fool of himself – and us, Dad warned Mam.

No he won't, will you? Mam asked uncertainly. Be a good lad, eh?

I will, Mam.

Huh, said Dad.

Don't keep frightening him, Mam pleaded.

Frighten him? Frighten *him*?

Pericles fidgets in his seat again, still managing to smile at the teacher although he has long since forgotten why he is smiling unless it is to encourage the pretty lady who smells of babysoap and who, from time to time, bathes him in a suspicious though not unfriendly glare. He rubs his boots together making them scream and Miss Hudson jumps.

'Who – ? Pericles – '

'Yes, ma'am?'

'In heaven's name – nothing. Be *quiet*!'

'Yes, ma'am.'

Damn fool, Dad said.

The old Austin coasted easily down the last hundred yards to the school, thumping in and out of ruts like a train shunting. Pericles's satchel slipped to the floor. Jesus, Dad said, and shook his head. Can't you sit still and not be dropping things.

Yes, Dad.

Yes, Dad, Dad mimicked.

Pericles picked Mam's velvet dress free of hairs at the shoulder and then retrieved her purse from the floor of the second-class carriage as the train stopped shunting and roared out of the station to take them away from the city and towards the coast where they would catch the ferry for home. As far as he could remember it was the only time he had ever known Mam to drop anything. Mam took the purse and continued to stare out of the window, saying nothing. There's not another thing I can tell you, I'm afraid, Mrs Stort, the doctor said sympathetically. You'll just have to be patient. As a city man he felt he should tell this unfortunate bewildered woman to have faith since it seemed fair medical practice, under the circumstances, to encourage the peasantry by administering a drop of the occult with the prescription. Instead he said: I honestly don't think there's a great deal for you to worry about. The boy is slow, of course, but I cannot see any reason why your husband should be so afraid of his turning violent. That seems highly unlikely in my view, although I'm not infallible. He heaved a short sigh by way of apology for this shortcoming. Naturally, I cannot foretell how he will react to any given situation, you understand. Quite often some seemingly insignificant occurrence which would not even register with us can trigger off an abnormal reaction in a patient and . . . He turned his palms upwards and shrugged. You do understand, Mrs Stort? Mam didn't of course, but she said politely: Yes, doctor, thank you. Time alone will tell, the doctor predicted and repeated this philosophy like a man who has waited all his life for time to tell him something.

Pericles wants to ask the teacher why time always seems to lie to him but decides to hold his silence since Grandad is trying to say something.

Had one just like this a long, long time ago, Grandad told him wistfully as he pared his nails with the boy's new knife, seeming to regret the weapon more than that of his vanished youth. Could nail a squirrel to a tree at a fair distance, I could. Ever tried throwing it, boy? Best defence a man ever had, silent and sure.

That's right, go on, teach him and it'll be one of us that ends up nailed to a bloody tree, you great fool, Dad bellowed.

We die when we die, Grandma wheezed from her chair by the stove, knowing they were all longing for her to go but determined to make a fight of it. We're only born to die, you know, she added, cackling.

Shit, Dad muttered under his breath.

Shit, said one of the twins and Dad hit him hard across the face.

Going fishing tomorrow. Want to come, boy? Grandad asked.

Yes, Grandad, Pericles said.

Bloody suit one another, Dad remarked. And stop that howling or I'll really give you something to howl about, he shouted, and the twin stopped howling abruptly.

Pericles watched the old man wade into the river and balance himself like the man by the weir on the calendar which hung for years behind the kitchen door, its pages dull-brown and brittle. Grandad held his poking stick in one hand, his net in the other, and the boy's knife in his belt. Pericles worried about the knife, about all the things that could happen to it. He hoped they would catch no fish. It would be acceptable if fish screamed or something before dying, or if they actually had to be killed: but they never cried out. Unaware, perhaps, of the finality of their situation they just suffocated. It seemed particularly cruel: just to flash silver and then smother. Drowned in the air, Grandad once said, and now he prodded his way along the bank with his long pole. Got a bugger, he shouted gleefully, and then he slipped.

Miss Hudson reads the story of the nativity in a sad voice, that modulated intonation filled with semi-quavers favoured by irregular Catholics for the recitation of the Stations of the Cross. The children follow each word with their grubby fingers in their own books as she reads aloud: But every door was closed against them – So, what do you intend to do now . . .? You can hardly expect *me* to . . . as for your father . . . anyway, everyone around here seems to know and they would only make it impossible for . . . much better get yourself a flat and . . . Tricia Hudson allows only fragments of her mother's self-protective tirade to penetrate her brain. She had expected little understanding from that quarter and, in truth, was relieved to find she was to get none. It was enough that her father understood, or at least appeared to. He had made a strange progression from slow horses whose performance was determined by the stars to equally obstinate thoroughbreds which were controlled by spiritual beings of indeterminate origin – invisible riders of the night, he once called them. The trick, no easy matter, was to identify the particular mystical jockey under whose influence a particular animal came. To help him in his search he had taken to spending his days in the public library absorbed in the works of McGregor Mathers, Eliphas Levi and Madame Blavatsky. It soon became quite impossible for him to talk of anything but the occult, posturing interminably about tarot, alchemy, Rosicrucianism and astral journeys. Indeed, he had just finished recounting his exploits on one such trip when Tricia decided to tell him of her pregnancy. There seemed little point in trying to minimize her predicament by euphemisms so she announced simply: I think you'd better know that I'm pregnant. His reaction was typically unpredictable. He was hugely delighted.

Marvellous, marvellous, marvellous, he exclaimed, jumping about the room, hugging himself and beaming delightedly. And the timing so right, he chuckled. So propitious! It will be a boy, of course.

Of course, she agreed, if you say so.

Oh, I do. Indeed I do. And you will call him Sefer.

Sefer? I don't know that I like that much.

No matter. Sefer it must be. Don't you understand?

Frankly, no.

Never mind. You will. When?

When what?

When will he be born?

Six months.

From now precisely?

Give or take a week.

March. Pisces. Marvellous. Sefer.

It might be a girl –

Rubbish. Oh, it's a boy. Don't you worry your pretty little head about that.

I'm not worried.

Good.

I just hope you won't be disappointed.

Good heavens! Why should I be?

Well, things have an odd way of not quite working out the

way *you* expect them to –

Not this time. Oh, no, not this time. You've made everything worthwhile, you wonderful child!

There's no answer to that.

March. Let me think. March, that's when we will all have our answer. My God, I can hardly wait!

Well, I'm sorry but I'm afraid you have to. I can hardly speed things up. Nature has a stubborn way of taking its own time.

No, oh no. The timing is perfect. Couldn't be better.

I'm glad you're pleased. I was worried you might –

Pleased? Pleased? What an understatement. How can I make you fathom the depth of my joy? There simply are no words that I know of.

I think I understand, Tricia lied kissing her father lightly on the cheek, suddenly embarrassed and saddened by the tears she saw welling up in his eyes.

The dog held its snout high and sniffed hungrily as they carried Grandad's bloated body into the farmhouse. They placed him on the table in the parlour and water seeped through the warps and plopped on the floor, forming puddles which were to mark the floor for ever. Grandma sat in her place by the stove in the kitchen poking erratically at the embers, unaware that her husband was dead and dripping on the parlour floor behind her: she would have scolded him severely for his untidiness had she noticed. Nobody but Mam seemed sorry that Grandad was dead.

Where's your Grandad, son, Mam asked, a little surprised to see the boy come home alone.

Pericles stared at her but said nothing.

You went out with him – where is he? Mam persisted.

Can't you answer your mother? Dad wanted to know.

Do you think he's had an accident? Mam asked Dad, alarmed.

Maybe. He's daft enough, Dad said obliquely and rounded on Pericles. Damn you, boy, he shouted. We'll go and find the old fool. Come on, Mike.

There, you've upset your father again, Pericles, Mam told him. Why can't you answer me when I ask you something? I just wish I knew what I have to do to get through to you.

Dad and Mike found Grandad all right, but it took them three days: Grandad's poking stick had become wedged between two rocks on the river bed and held him under. When they pried him loose and he floated to the surface he still gripped the pole in one hand and his net in the other, but he no longer looked anything like the man in the calendar. Pericles smiled quietly to himself.

'I wonder if any of you can understand what it must be like to feel totally abandoned,' Miss Hudson wonders, smiling balefully at the children. 'Can you imagine the feeling of knowing that nobody, nobody at all wants you?'

Feel this, said Big Mike invitingly as someone in another room muttered nonsense in their sleep.

What are you asking him to feel? Vigy demanded urgently.

Aw, shut it, growled Big Mike and covered his own and Pericles' head with the blanket. Feel this, he said again quickly, and placed the boy's hand on his long, hard organ. Pericles enjoyed the feel of his brother's warmth.

Big Mike, you just stop asking him to do that, Vigy warned grimly.

The admixture of veins and muscle throbbed gently in Pericles' hand. Then it jerked and spewed out stickiness which felt as warm as milk on his fingers. Big Mike, can I ask you something?

What?

Could I do that?

Naw, said Big Mike lazily: he was tired and comfortable now.

But alone and in secret Pericles tried it and found that he could.

The clock is suddenly functioning in his brain again now. He slides to the very edge of the desk and watches Miss Hudson as she reads from a small book. He hears her mention little Jesus and little shepherd boys and little stars.

Very little else we can do for the moment, said the doctor kindly.

Mam sighed. Maybe there's some pills – ?

Hardly, said the thrush and whirred benignly. We could, of course, if you wanted it, send him to an institution.

Oh, no, said Mam, alarmed. Oh, no, not that.

I must say I agree with you. There's absolutely no reason for such a drastic step at the moment. But if you find that in time you –

Pericles watched Mam prepare for the funeral. Grandma prepared also. Somehow they had made her understand the calamity and she passed the time tuning up her wails. Grandma needed time to perfect things but when the time came she would perform adequately: she was now very old and very slow but everything she put her mind to she did thoroughly.

Pericles heard his sisters giggle as they tore up old newspapers and swabbed Grandad down.

Wash your hands before you eat, Grandma ordered: it was the first command any of them could remember her issuing so they obeyed her without question.

Somewhere a bell is ringing. The lead cow heaved her bulk slowly from the fields her great udder swaying, her bell tolling monotonously. And Mam rang the cracked bell to get them out of bed. The bell persists. Miss Hudson rings the school bell vigorously. With shouts of delight the children herd from the classroom, galloping away like colts as soon as they leave the teacher's sight. Pericles prepares to go home also, his satchel securely tucked under his arm.

'Pericles – ' Miss Hudson calls tentatively.

'Yes, ma'am?'

'Just one moment. Come here please,' advancing a little herself. 'I want a word with you.'

The boy remains motionless: it seems futile to go to the teacher since she appears bent on coming to him.

'Pericles,' begins Miss Hudson adopting a strict tone but abandoning it after only the one word. 'Pericles, you – what I'm trying to tell you is that what you did today – I don't want to seem unfair or unreasonable – what you did was really very wrong, you know that, don't you?'

'Yes, ma'am,' admits Pericles, generously prepared to agree to anything for the moment.

'Then tell me – why, why *did* you do it – ?'

Just let me *feel* you, said Poppy Burn. I won't *eat* you.

Pericles shrugs.

Miss Hudson blows chalk-dust from her dainty fingers daintily.

Feel this, said Big Mike.

Pericles smells the teacher's babysoap and likes it again. He likes Miss Hudson, he decides. Likes her better than anyone else he knows. He watches her intently, waiting.

Oh, Lord, Tricia Hudson tells herself, what a strange impossible child. But there is nothing peevish in her thought. She feels a great surge of affection for the boy and is somehow frightened by this. Of course it's frightening, quoth the idiot quack, when the last thing she wanted was to be agreed with. As if anyone could understand the sheer blind terror of finding oneself sweating and trembling and fully clothed and sitting in an empty bath waiting to be cleansed while for some obscure reason one had chosen to ignore the taps and merely flushed the toilet instead. And she had remained helplessly in the bath allowing the liquid Radox to seep herbally into her dress while she stared at the minute cracks in the plaster on the wall like the lines on an old woman's face. Suddenly she began trembling violently in every limb. But it was not the ludicrous situation in which she found herself that terrified her. It was simply that all at once every tiny sound in the room lurched to an horrific crescendo. It was as if, and it was this which flayed her battered

45

mind most appallingly, it was as if every scream was part of herself, a sad and abandoned part irredeemably cast adrift to fend for itself.

'There must have been a reason, Pericles.'

'Yes, ma'am' agrees Pericles. He hears the bird in the clock. Hears Grandad's screams. The little fox chewed the bones and eyed him.

Someone calls his name from the yard outside: it sounds like Dad but it could be Big Mike who sounds a lot like Dad when he shouts. 'Ah. Someone is here to collect you,' Miss Hudson tells him. 'You'd better run along now. We'll say no more about what happened,' and once again she puffs chalk-dust from her finger-tips.

Pericles climbs in beside Dad or Big Mike, his satchel under his arm. Pericles climbed into the truck beside Dad or Big Mike, his satchel under his arm. The truck capered over the stones someone had placed in the mud and sometimes pitched high in the air, the bonnet flapping. The piece of wire holding the metal down would have to be tightened again.

– not dangerous, said the doctor, and the train whooshed into the tunnel and out again screaming as the driver played with his whistle.

We'll pray, said Ma, happy to delegate responsibility to God.

Shit, said Dad.

Take more than prayer with that one, decided Big Mike. Take a bloody miracle.

I'll pray anyway, said Mam firmly.

And I'll pray too, said Grandma from beside the stove for no reason.

Thank you, Grandma, said Mam.

Shit, said Dad again but quietly, wary of the barrage of incantation being mustered against him.

Pericles sat in the truck enjoying the ride and he sits in the truck and enjoys the ride. The winter sun shines thinly as though reflected from a pond instead of beaming directly from

46

the sky. The hedges gather up their roots and bundle their raw ugly branches past him. The gaunt trees ease their stiff, naked branches in heavy slumber. The old truck farts like Grandad after pulses.

Don't just sit there, Pericles, Mam snapped unexpectedly. Get up and do something useful.

Like what, Mam?

Anything.

Dad spat.

He always looks at me funny when you're here, Mam told Dad. It gives me the willies.

Pray then, retorted Dad, and laughed.

Don't mock, Mam scolded.

You'll need to shout, though, if you want anyone to hear prayers for him.

Grandad shouted for him to get help but Pericles stayed on the bank and watched him drown. Once he almost did help the old man but changed his mind and crouched down the closer to study the grim process of death. Justice appeared to be taking place: Grandad always suffocated the fish in air but now they had turned the tables. How they had contrived this was a mystery but wonderful nonetheless. Grandad's bloated body even stank of fish as it lay in the parlour and twitched each time the door was slammed.

Pericles watched Miss Hudson's breasts twitch as she stretched to create the moon.

'Well, what did you learn today, professor?' asks Dad or Big Mike.

Pericles reached out his hand and touched the teacher's bottom gently, smiling.

And this is the Virgin Mary.

'Lost your tongue, boy?'

I'll show you the lot of me one day, Poppy Burn promised, shaking her long hair seductively in his face. But she didn't smell of babysoap.

47

'Jesus Christ, are you deaf or something?'

Pericles stares out of the truck as it careers into the farmyard scattering chickens and ducks while the dog snaps stupidly at the front tyres. He has already made up his mind to swop his jacket for his old woollen jersey, his satchel for his knife. What he will do then he has not yet decided.

'Can't you answer a simple question, boy?'

One good thing, Dad announced, that murderous knife is gone for good.

Pericles smiled quietly.

What did you learn today, professor? someone asked.

Pericles smiles quietly. 'Plenty,' he says. He is getting on famously.

Spring

From a winter as dark as the House of Usher spring emerged slowly on the island. Then, almost overnight, buds appeared on the trees, primroses lined the hedgerows, and rooks scavenged noisily for twigs. Old people sighed with relief now that their critical time of year had overlooked them and they tightened their faces to cope with the year ahead.

Pericles copies into his exercise book everything that the teacher writes on the blackboard. His letters weave alarmingly but the words are legible enough and he makes no mistakes. Pericles likes writing. Miss Hudson moves easily from child to child, leaning over each, correcting, encouraging, chiding, praising. She leans over Pericles, who pretends not to notice her but smiles inwardly and writes on. Such a fish! he writes carefully, shining silver from head to tail, and here and there a crimson dot; with a grand hooked nose, and grand curling lip, and grand bright eye, looking round him proudly as a king, and surveying the water right and left as if it all belonged to him . . . Today we'll practise our writing with a passage from the Water Babies, Miss Hudson said. You remember I read you some of it yesterday.

When the thrush whirrs obediently for Joseph Butterworth everyone leaves the classroom: they gather in small groups in the play-yard. Pericles stands alone and watches, amused at the covert glances in his direction. Then, as the children line up he lines up also. One after another they disappear into the shed. When his turn comes Pericles goes into the shed and masters his buttons. In the urinal lies a square inch of mauve disinfectant: he aims most carefully at this. Then someone shouts: hurry up,

will you, I'm bursting. Pericles tucks his pickle away comfortably and is very fastidious about holing his buttons.

Back in the classroom he writes again, and listens attentively,
and writes some more: Tom was so frightened that he longed to
creep into a hole; but he need not have been; for salmon are all
true gentlemen, and, like true gentlemen, they look noble and
proud enough, but go about their own business, and leave rude
fellows to themselves . . . Miss Hudson leans over him, one
dainty hand resting on his shoulder lightly.

Got one, said Grandad, and then he slipped.

'Why, that is excellent, Pericles,' says the teacher, delighted
with his/her progress, while Pericles writes on laboriously.
'Your writing is quite beautiful, Pericles. Well done.'

Beautiful Pericles, said the teacher.

An expectant silence falls over the classroom as Father Denis
Redmond appears in the doorway. He has come to hear the
catechism. Each child stands to answer in turn, rattling out
words learned by heart and meaning very little to them. Father
Redmond seems to lose track of the proceedings somewhere
along the way and discontinues his questions after only five,
launching instead into a short confusing sermon on the Trinity.

Pericles listens without too much interest.

'We have God the Father, God the Son and God the Holy
Ghost,' the priest appears mildly embarrassed to tell them.

You know it really is a bit preposterous, Father Redmond
told the bishop or some stray canon who had unwittingly
allowed himself to be cornered, it really is not too far short of
outrageous. I mean it's hard enough, don't you think, to avoid
the wrath – or at least dodge it occasionally – of one God
without having to sidestep the anger of three . . . But whoever
he had trapped had disagreed with this heresy and he found
himself in the throes of a lukewarm argument with himself,
knowing the result would be total agreement with himself. The
inner ferment within him, occasionally quelled by some witty
aside, was held in check; the squalls and eddies of jangled fear

would return, he knew, only when, sober (as he would un-doubtedly be, he assured himself) he would have to ascend the altar and commence the incantation of an archaic and, in his case, garbled liturgy which had long since ceased to uplift him. Perhaps it was the statutory hallowed gloom of his church, of all churches for that matter, which brought about the inevit-able melancholy. Places of the late and deadly night, he had once described them to a startled congregation, places where diabolic rather than glorious plans were hatched. They hadn't liked that, had walked out and left him high and dry (dry! particularly dry) in the sumptuously carved pulpit, near to tears, feeling the church's gloom and doom wrap itself around him with its certainty of sorrow and penitence and suffering. Christ? Are You there? he had screamed in the echoing empty cave of worship, can You hear me?

'Goodbye, Father,' shout the children in chorus.

'Goodbye, children,' replies Father Redmond. 'God bless each and every one of you.'

'Goodbye, Father,' says Miss Hudson. Or: go to hell, then, she shouted at the smug voice behind the protective wire-mesh grille, furious at her own vulgarity and more than a little concerned at what restitution God might exact for her im-passioned outburst. Bless me father for I have sinned – on the face of it facile enough patter, but it had taken, she felt, great courage and humility on her part to utter those seven words; well aware though she was, erect and impenitent in the con-fessional, that she was guilty of inverted pride. Which, after all was said and done, was not such a bad thing, really, was it, for pride, under whatever guise, forced one to go on and be smothered by ancient incomprehensible doctrines, or to flaunt sin in the face of God. As for the devil, well, he was beside her and in front of her and behind her and inside her it was implied, docile enough for the moment, otherwise occupied, perhaps even taking forty winks. It had been a grotesque encounter:

Are you sincerely sorry for this terrible sin, my child?

I'm sorry, of course, father, but I don't think it was all *that* terrible.

Not *that* terrible? Oh, child, what can you be saying? You have sinned even against the Virgin herself. Hell fire and utter damnation stares you in the face and all you can say is that it's not that –

Really, father, I can't believe that just because I –

Just because you –

I said I was sorry.

Oh, but you're not, young woman. You pride yourself in your awful arrogance –

I *am* sorry –

You don't even know what the word means!

Don't I just. I can tell you I know I'm damn sorry I'm four months pregnant –

Aaah, the voice wailed.

And I was sorry enough to come and confess –

Without true contrition –

And now I'm truly sorry that I bothered to come here at all and have to listen to you blathering about –

And what about God Almighty?

What about God Almighty?

It is God you have offended.

I *know* that. Although He's probably laughing His head off right now listening to –

How dare you!

Easily –

Do you promise never to offend our Blessed Lord again by committing this most heinous sin?

Well, I'm certainly not going to go racing about looking for ways to upset Him, if that's what you mean.

Don't be flippant.

I was answering your stupid question.

You positively refuse to realize that your immortal soul is in the most terrible peril.

Oh, for heaven's sake, father.

Yes – for heaven's sake you must –

Oh, don't be so damned dramatic. I'm sorry – I shouldn't have –

Leave the confessional this instant, you wicked woman.

I want absolution –

Not from me. From me you will get nothing until you learn humility, until you crawl before the sight of God and beg for forgiveness on your knees.

Well, go to hell then.

Pericles hands his copybook to the teacher who stands at her rostrum and gathers the books for correction. Beautiful Pericles, said Miss Hudson. Tomorrow he will get his copybook back marked in blue, mistakes underlined in red. He listens for the thrush.

'The bell has gone, Pericles. You must go home now,' Miss Hudson tells him, putting her babysoap-scented hand on his shoulder.

'Yes, ma'am,' says Pericles. He tucks the satchel snugly under his arm and fastens the centre button of his jacket carefully.

Open them carefully, Mam warned. Don't just jerk the buttons off, she added shaking a finger at him.

Don't jerk off. Haw! guffawed Big Mike.

Shut your dirty mouth, shouted Dad, but he smiled all the same.

He gets dirtier every day, Mam complained. I wish you'd deal with him.

He's a man now, Dad explained. He deals with himself. Be better if you let *that* boy grow up too.

He will. In his own good time.

'I'll see you tomorrow,' says Miss Hudson. 'You've been a very good boy today.'

'Yes, ma'am. Bye, ma'am.'

Say ma'am to the teacher, Mam told him. She's a lady and

you've got to respect her.

Yes, Mam, said Pericles and stretched out his hand and touched the lady's bottom gently.

That's a good boy.

You're wasting your time talking to that moron, Dad told her and shook his head.

I am not, Mam insisted. He always does what I ask him to. He's a good boy.

Shit.

You're the cause of all the trouble.

Me? Me? What have I done now, woman?

Shouting at him all the time the way you do. You only make the poor child worse.

Worse, indeed. How could he be any worse than he is, would you mind telling me?

He's been no trouble at all lately, Mam defended him. School could do him a lot of good if you'd just leave him be.

Pericles hangs on tightly to his satchel and places his feet with exaggerated care on the stepping stones in the lane. The sun has been hanging long enough in the sky to dry itself out and is trying, now, to do the same for the earth. The hedges and trees are almost green again and everything that seemed dead in the winter months has discovered enormous energy. You watch your boots, Dad warned. Can't go getting you new boots every day of the week.

You didn't get him those, Mam said. Big Mike gave them to him and *he* got them from poor Aunt Girlie.

Well, he better look after them, Dad insisted, because I've got no money to be buying him new ones.

It is very quiet, the lazy, satisfied quiet that small birds and invisible insects make. Pericles picks a blade of fresh dustless grass and chews it, sucking the juice.

As he comes into the farmyard the dog yaps at him hoarsely. Mam waves a cloth from an upstairs window and calls: 'You're home safe and sound. Good.'

Pericles waves back to his mother but she has vanished from the window and by the time he reaches the back door he can hear her rattling pans and plates, and he knows he will be expected to eat. The dog hopes the same and rushes ahead of him into the kitchen. Grandad had certainly looked funny all dressed up in his best black suit and stretched out on the parlour table, candles set about him at intervals to form a flickering cross. And this is Jesus who died on the cross to save us, somebody told him.

'Eat this, Pericles,' Mam told him. 'There's more turnip in the oven if you want it.'

'Thanks, Mam.'

'A healthy body makes a healthy mind,' Mam tells him.

' – ?'

' – so eat up everything,' she adds smiling.

'Yes, Mam.'

'And wash your plate for me when you're finished, will you? I have to go up and get on with the cleaning. Where all the dust comes from I'll never know.'

'I will, Mam.'

'Good boy. I wish the rest of them were half as good as you,' Mam sighs, coming over to him and kissing his hair. 'My life would be so much easier if they were.'

Mam smells of polish and the liquid stuff she squirts on the windows once a month.

Pericles eats, runs the tap on his plate, and gives the scraps to the waiting dog. Small neat piles. 'Here,' he says.

The fox slid off decapitated.

Pericles bends down and strokes the dog but, once fed, the brute becomes surly and moves off to lie in the sun. Pericles walks across the yard and into the cornfield on his way to the river.

We'll get on famously, said the teacher.

Oh, yes, ma'am, he agreed readily.

I knew we would.

He studies the still-green and stocky corn and wonders why Dad likes to have it cut when it is golden and most beautiful, leaving the field shorn and ragged. He must ask Big Mike. The field is very placid just now: there is no breeze and the green stems are erect and stiff, busily sucking nourishment from the earth. A bird shoots high into the air above him, cavorts wildly, whistles, vanishes before his very eyes. Pericles stops to think about this, but something happens. He is back in the wooden shed in the play-yard and is urinating again. From behind the shed there comes a thumping noise and then what sounds like paper being torn in the same way Vigy tears it when she's finished: with great precision as though making a design. But Vigy doesn't go to school any more. Vigy has a 'proper' job in the canning factory near the little harbour where she makes sure only the best fruit gets through. So who tore the paper, and why? He would look closer next time and maybe he would discover something new. His heart beats faster: if there is one thing Pericles likes more than anything else it is the sense of discovery: getting something new, as he puts it.

Let me feel, said Poppy Burn. And she did and he grasped her fat meaty buttocks.

He was playing with her bottom and is playing with himself and wondering at his erection. Big Mike's advice would be needed again since he knew everything.

Pericles felt excited as he honed the knife and listened to Mam's final instructions most attentively. Bend its head back, she told him demonstrating with her wrist, and then slit the throat clean. Just one clean cut – that's all it takes, and let the blood run out.

You're not letting that fool loose with his knife, are you? Dad asked in alarm.

Mam ignored him: you remember what I told you? she asked Pericles.

Yes, Mam.

Well, go on then. Off you go and show me what a clever boy

you are.

Pericles followed Mam's instructions to the letter and slit the chicken's throat cleanly, enjoying the feel of warm blood running down his hand.

Feel this, whispered Big Mike urgently.

Pericles bent back the neck of another chicken and slit its gizzard. Then another. And another.

Jesus Christ! roared Dad – stop that fucking maniac before he slaughters every bird we've got.

I'm not going near him, Big Mike said, backing off.

Don't just stand there gaping, Dad roared again to nobody in particular.

You do something, Big Mike told Dad. I'm bloody well keeping clear of him.

Pericles happily continued his massacre.

That's your goddam clever little boy for you, Dad shouted at Mam. You told him to do it – now you can try and stop him.

Pericles! Stop! Mam called shrilly.

And Pericles stopped. He stared first at Mam and then at the havoc about him. He was amazed to see that he had killed more than one bird. He could remember only the first. He felt sorry for the dead chickens scattered about him, their white plumage speckled with blood although, somehow, they looked prettier now. Then he ran, ran from Dad who galloped after him wielding the forked pole Mam used to keep the centre of the clothes-line up. Pericles hid himself well, and once he felt secure he wiped the blood from the knife by running his tongue along the blade. Then he licked each finger clean in turn.

Standing on the stone wall surrounding the corn field Pericles stares about him. He hears Mam scream for Dad to stop beating him, and at the same time he feels the teacher's buttocks as she whispers beautiful Pericles. She has soft, soft buttocks and even softer breasts he notices as she opens her blouse and leans over him to admire his writing. Only one button remains closed and he helps her with that. Her breasts have little splashes of blood on each pinnacle and he licks them clean for her. Beautiful, Pericles, we'll get on famously.

Pericles jumps down from the wall, leans against it and scuffs one foot in the clay.

The little fox remained crucified in the yard for three days and three nights drying, perhaps for the sins of the world. The red fur of the brush and the delicate dainty paws became hard and ugly as blood clotted and dried in them.

Git, said Grandma, and the dog slunk from the kitchen.

Grandad's dead, remarked one of the twins. Pericles drownded him, he added.

Help, Grandad screamed. Damn you, boy. Help.

Pericles waited until the old man had been under the water for a long time before he decided to investigate. He waded carefully into the river and pulled the body through the reeds and on to the bank. Then he retrieved his knife from Grandad's belt and cleaned it carefully, drying it meticulously on his trousers. Satisfied, he just sat beside the body and stared at it hopelessly. The fear of dying made Grandad's face look horrible: it was twisted in terror and Pericles was suddenly ashamed of the old man. He sensed there was something wrong in his shame and decided to protect Mam from feeling the same way. He wouldn't let her see Grandad's face. He pushed the body back into the water and wedged it securely under the poking rod. Finally, he sat on the bank again and caressed his knife and polished it up nicely.

One good thing, Dad said, perhaps trying in his clumsy way to rid his mind of the inevitability of death, that murderous bloody knife is gone for good and all.

Pericles smiles quietly as he had smiled quietly.

When they were all exhausted and had fallen fitfully asleep, Pericles crept downstairs. It was very quiet except for Big Mike who had probably done himself again and was snoring loudly. Occasionally Vigy moaned, and once the baby whimpered like a pup that had just been weaned. Pericles came stealthily into the parlour and stared in silent anger and disbelief at the corpse on the table not yet dapperly dressed for burial. He wiped his knife back and forth on his palm, thinking. Then he reached out and prodded the body tentatively: Grandad shivered and his eyelids seemed to flicker but the awful expression on his face did not change. Pericles prodded the bloated body again trying to figure something out. Perhaps if he let the water out and gave Grandad back his proper shape Mam would not be so upset. Yes, that seemed reasonable enough. The colourless liquid oozed very slowly from the new gash in the thigh but the body remained gross and misshapen. Perhaps a larger opening was needed. Pericles stabbed the corpse in a frenzy of expectancy. The chest, the throat, the belly and thighs were lacerated but Grandad refused to co-operate and remained swollen and enormous, still with that look of disbelieving terror and reproach on his face.

Get up! Pericles shouted. Get up, damn you.

Pericles finds he has arrived at the river: he takes off his boots and lets his feet dangle in the water.

He was still shouting for the old man to get up when Dad and Big Mike pulled him away and locked him in an outside shed.

That's it, Dad roared thumping the table and making the mugs jump. That is bloody well it. We'll have to get that mad bastard locked up. It could have been any one of us he made into mincemeat, he shouted. And we'd have been asleep and not known we'd been killed, he added as though that made matters worse.

Mam rocked herself in her chair and wept.

Pericles drownded Grandad and then made him into mincemeat, one of the twins announced admiringly.

We should have known it would come to this, Big Mike acknowledged decisively. First the chickens and now –

Hush, Mam pleaded. Nobody need know of this. The doctor and Sergeant Bullock have both agreed he died by accident in the river. I'll fix him up so nobody need know.

Are you out of your mind, woman? Dad asked wildly. We can't just go on and pretend it never happened.

No, we don't have to pretend it never happened, Mam agreed, but we needn't *tell* anyone about it. They'll only come and take him away from me.

That'd be the best thing that ever happened. We wouldn't have to be looking over our shoulder every five minutes.

He wouldn't do it to *us*, Mam said, sounding shocked.

You didn't think he'd do it to Grandad, did you, but he did.

I won't let them take him away from me, Mam said, her voice rising.

Dad suddenly found himself unable to cope: Oh, have it your own way, woman. But if Bullock finds out and comes after us or if anything else happens it'll be on your head. I'm finished with him.

But Dad wasn't quite finished with him it seemed. Pericles managed to escape from the shed and hid for two whole days and nights before Dad finally caught up with him and whipped him unmercifully. Then he tied his hands behind his back and padlocked a length of chain about his neck and linked this to a staple in the cowshed, and he was left there until the day after the funeral. Alone and in darkness Pericles managed to lick the whip-wounds on his shoulders and felt better: maybe that was what he should have done to bring Grandad back.

Pericles stares at his feet in the water, moving them back and forth: they have taken on an odd shape, like large white pike. Proper gentlemen.

That was your brother, Dad told Mam, coming into the kitchen from the telephone. He says we should have him done by the priest.

Done?

Exorcised or something.

Oh, no, Mam exclaimed, terrified.

Why the hell not? asked Dad. It's the only damn thing we haven't tried.

We could surely try it, encouraged Big Mike.

Oh, no, wailed Mam again.

Well, it's either that or the madhouse, Dad told her firmly, the strange promise of occult assistance giving him courage. I'm not having him running about loose the way he is. I should have reported it to Bullock in the first place only you talked me out of it.

You *couldn't*, Mam insisted. Not our own child.

He's not even our – Dad started. Anway, I've made up my mind. I'm going to ask the priest tomorrow. He's mad enough himself to know what to do.

Don't say that, Bill, Mam pleaded.

Good, that's settled, said Big Mike, looking forward to this new experience.

Exorcized? Father Redmond asked astounded, looking from the man to the boy beside him and away again quickly. Like the truth he found the child well nigh impossible to face. He wanted nothing whatsoever to do with this situation, least of all to tamper with what he clearly recognized as childish ignorance if not plain innocence. Immediately, though, he knew he was going to get himself talked into it.

It's for the child's sake, someone said to him.

I suppose it is, Father Redmond agreed, supposing nothing of the sort, and he felt himself beginning to believe the lie. He had, he could acknowledge graciously, lied on so many occasions to so many phantoms that there no longer existed a firm basis for his self-deception.

You're our only hope, Father. If you can't do something we'll have to get him locked away.

Oh, you can cure him, Father. I know you can, the woman said.

– ?

Isn't there something you say that makes them all right? Them?

Oh, you can cure him, the woman said again.

– get him locked up in a madhouse, penetrated Father Redmond's mind.

There was something in the rugged uncomplicated faith of these people which he knew he would never be able to withstand, a trust born of that once-familiar, undemanding belief, that forgotten passport to courage and dignity, the desire to do what was good and right and proper. It was as though, suddenly, he had stopped deceiving himself, had stopped lying back to those lying factions. And he badly needed a drink.

Perhaps I could try, he conceded. Which was all very well but who was *I*, where had *I* gone, how to assume *I*? Nonetheless, whatever *I* did, he decided, *I* would do with charm and dignity, and with considerable charm and dignity he accepted the tumbler of whiskey and drank. After the fourth drink he hardly heard the voices around him, could not tell if he was answering their questions or not (if, indeed, they were asking any). He was aware, however, that even as the occasion for desperate honesty was receding, advancing was what he could only hope was his own salvation, borne on the shoulders of this pathetic child.

Right this minute? he heard himself ask horror-stricken.

Why not, Father?

I can't very well do it just now, can I? And his panic might have been less had not the wretched man chosen that precise moment to screw the cap firmly on to the whiskey bottle again.

Can I? he asked again, casually holding out his glass.

Whenever it is convenient to you, Father, the woman told him.

Convenience has nothing whatever to do with it, he thought he heard himself say but probably hadn't, had obviously said something quite different since the man, overlooking the empty outstretched glass, overlooking, too, the desperate anxiety in Father Redmond's eyes, was telling him: Yes, that will be fine, Father. We'll have everything ready for you then.

Oh, Holy God . . . Father Redmond made a supreme effort

and assumed an expression intended to be compassionate but nonetheless indicative of total clerical sanity. But he was in very deep water. And without the requisite paddle. Hounds of Hell trundled their great padded paws about his brain. Fortunately, he was always on the alert for something of this nature and was now almost adequately prepared for it. The hounds of hell are silly shapes of sin, they shrivel at the word, he was saying with bland irrelevance, oblivious to the bewilderment it caused. I knew a hound of hell once, he continued gaily, a desperate brute called Kimmy – an afanc of monstrous proportions. Although, on reflection, which is what I'm trying to do now, reflect I mean, I don't suppose he was – a hound of hell, that is – since no word shrivelled him. Nor sin either (he knew he was beginning to rant stupidly), more's the pity.

  – ?

If only it did! If only we could pluck some delectable word from the air, utter it, and remove our own sins! But what would be the point, he concluded with complete seriousness, of forgiving ourselves?

  – ?

  – ?

There was a legend, you know, among the whatever they call them in Borneo, or maybe it was the Aborigines of Tasmania – did you know they once had Aborigines in Tasmania? Where was I – ah, yes, a legend that God didn't really want to be bothered with us at all. It was up to *us*, you see, to attract *His* attention by whistling and dancing and singing and, I shouldn't wonder, throwing in the odd yoo-hoo and a bang on the big bass drum –

Yes, Father. Well now –

– but what actually happened when you finally got His benevolent eye focused on you I have no idea.

Father –

I suppose you just waited until He was distracted and started the whole process over again, Father Redmond smiled wistfully and shook the empty glass in his hand. What was that you said?

Would Thursday suit you, Father?

Thursday? Suit? For what?

To – you know – to – the boy.

Ah, the boy. Hmm, what are we going to do with you?

Dad glanced at Mam and raised his eyes to the ceiling: I thought we'd arranged and decided that, Father.

But we have. We have indeed, Haven't we? Father Redmond winked at the boy and Pericles smiled back as though they were sharing an enormously funny conspiratorial joke.

Good, said the man.

Thank you *very* much, Father, said the woman. If you need us to have anything special ready you can let us know.

Special? Father Redmond asked eyeing the mantlepiece on which the corked whiskey-bottle now stood.

Yes. Like – well I don't really know what you might need, do I?

Well, Father Redmond beamed, perhaps a little – these things can be a considerable strain, he indicated the bottle with correct vagueness.

There'll be as much of that as you might need, Father, the man told him. There's any amount left over from the funeral.

Funeral?

My father, the woman told him.

– ?

You buried him, Father.

I did?

The old man who drowned, the man added.

Ah, yes, I seem to remember.

– and I'll have a nice hot meal fixed up for you, the woman was assuring him.

Father Redmond felt his spirits rise considerably. How very kind you all are, he told them.

64

'Till Thursday then, Father.

Thursday? Oh. Yes. Admirable. I'll see you all then, then.

Pericles feels very peaceful here on the river bank with his feet in the water. He lies back and decides to doze, leaving his feet where they are and folding his arms behind his head. He picked up his mother's purse from the floor of the carriage and watched the hedges sheer away from the piercing whistle. Nobody spoke to him when he got up and left the classroom quickly but he wet himself anyway. Nobody spoke to him on Thursday either as they made him kneel in front of the priest and backed away. He felt very stupid on his knees but he stayed there for a long time since nobody thought to tell him to get up until long after the priest had finished whatever it was he had wanted to do. A lot of holy water had been splashed about him and a crucifix was waved in front of his face while Father Redmond roared strange prayers and looked comical in his dedevilling robes. Still, they had all been very nice to him for several weeks afterwards and even Dad shouted at him less.

Pericles thinks he will stop dozing soon and start to sleep properly.

Thank you for everything, Father. He's looking better already, isn't he Bill?

Dad was dubious: If you think so, he allowed.

The sun has started to slide behind the clouds which presage rain, but it is still quite warm. Pericles feels content, his feet cool, his body rested and relaxed, and he decides to wake up slowly. For some reason by the time he is fully awake the sky has turned blue-black and is dotted with stars like the ones borrowed by the teacher to decorate the blackboard, like the dress Mam wore when they finally buried Grandad, and shiny like that too. The stars are still tiny, but Pericles reaches out his hands as if to touch them. He has extraordinary hands: capable of great gentleness but equally capable of unscrewing two rusted drainwater pipes.

Vigy, just you come here this instant and help me, Mam

called. She had ordered the blue-black dress from a catalogue which Vigy had sent for and it fitted badly. It was now caught at her hips and Mam was scared she would tear it. I never should have bought this without trying it on, she complained out loud to herself.

I'll never get my hair done, Vigy called back. Can't you hang on just a minute?

Never mind your hair. You can run a comb through that in a second. Come here when I tell you.

There! said Vigy as she finally forced the dress into position.

Thanks, Vigy. It doesn't look too bad, does it?

You look grand, Mam.

What a terrible thing to happen, Mam said.

It's perfect now, Mam. Don't be silly.

Not the dress, Vigy. That's fine. Your Grandfather, I mean.

Oh.

I'm so thankful to God that nobody outside the family saw the dreadful mess he was in.

And later to Dad she said: I simply cannot understand what made the boy slash him up like that.

He's a murderous idiot, Dad muttered, fastening his braces.

But he so liked his Grandad, Mam insisted.

I've told you a thousand times, he's like a wild animal. He likes nobody, Dad told her yet again, arching his back and stretching painfully. His rheumatism was at its worst this time of year. (Youngsters grow and we old ones shrink and that's what causes the pain, Grandma explained. The shrinking brings the pain. It's a sign we're dying when we start to shrink, she persisted mournfully. And Dad glared at her as if he could cheerfully throttle her and said Shit!) Mean, that's what he is, Dad continued, shaking his finger at Mam. Mean and bloody dangerous, you mark my words.

He *can't* be, Mam said. He can be so gentle –

Gentle be damned. He should stay chained up in the cow-shed the way he is now.

66

Bill!

Stay that way for the rest of his natural life, if you ask me, Dad insisted.

Bill! Mam exclaimed again. It was always a sign of her agitation when she used her husband's first name instead of calling him Dad.

Evil, Dad insisted.

But you can't just leave him tied up –

Best place for him. Out of harm's way.

But it's so cruel. He's not an animal.

I tell you he is. Let him loose and the Lord alone knows what sort of trouble he'll land us in. I can tell you one thing – next time I'm calling Bullock so the police can deal with it or we'll be finding ourselves behind bars.

There won't be a next time, Mam insisted optimistically. Just you stop that kind of talk, Bill. You're making yourself believe things.

I can tell you one thing – he stays where he is until that priest of yours is done with him, I promise you that, Dad promised adamantly.

I suppose that could be best, Mam conceded.

Damn right it would. Are you ready? It's not a bloody wedding you're going to, you know.

I like to look my best. It's part of respect.

Well past your best you are and no mistake.

Mam stared at him and said nothing for the moment. But she defiantly slapped powder on her face just the same, using a huge circular puff shorn by years of wear, and dabbed a spot of eau-de-cologne behind each ear for good measure. Then she stalked out of the room throwing, You're not wearing so well yourself, over her shoulder. (Glory, glory, glory but you are the most beautiful girl I have ever set eyes on, young Mister Patrick Bullock told young Miss Eileen Ferris and held her hand as they sat on the cliff and stared out across the Atlantic, their hearts heaving like the ocean. But that had been so long, so long ago;

long before he went to Dublin and joined the police force and
became one of her sweet, misty memories, a memory kept alive
and vibrant by intricate strategies of her own devising. And
now, after all that time, he had returned to the island as its
solitary law-enforcer and Mam found herself avoiding him as
much as was possible in such a small community, hiding from
him the sadness she felt at the loss of her own beauty, hiding the
pain she felt as she noted how her lovely man had changed, his
fine young face all thickened and turned a mottled purple-red,
gone heavy and sagging and coarse as though determined to
bear witness to his name. It sometimes frightened her to realise
that for so long she had carried in her mind the image of how he
used to be, had irrationally presumed that the love they had
once shared would preserve and protect them both from the
ravages of time and care and worry and sadness. And in a sense
it had done just that for Eileen Stort: it had kept her spirit quite
young, reasonably gay, and usually good-natured. Eileen Stort
was not a stupid woman: she had great practical sense and a
bright imagination, and she had manipulated her fantasies so
successfully that she could transfer that strange tender emotion
– perhaps made gentler by the harshness of the surroundings –
she had shared with Patrick Bullock to her husband, her
children and, in particular, to Pericles – her lovely boy as she
liked to call him.)

It's you that's worn me out, said Dad, devilment dancing in
his eyes.

Pericles could see quite well through the window of the
cowshed despite the cobwebs and the grime on the glass. They
stood about the hearse, chatting solemnly, as Mike Young and
Peter Perrin heaved the coffin into position and placed the few
wreaths on top of it carefully, arranging the flowers artistically
and with a delicacy which one might have considered foreign to
such hard and unsentimental men. Thud. Grandad shifted
uneasily in the box, protesting to the bitter end. Oh, mind his
poor head, Mam pleaded suddenly. They all turned and gaped

at her; all except Sergeant Bullock who seemed to understand that death did not necessarily mean the end of pain, and who seemed about to go to Mam and comfort her but changed his mind, looked away, and flicked some invisible object from the lapel of his neatly pressed uniform. Then Mam started to cry and it looked, this time, as though Dad was about to go to her but he, too, changed his mind. Let's get moving, men, he said.

Mam still seemed to be sobbing when she came to release him. Pericles could not fully understand her tears but he felt deeply sorry for her, sorry, too, that things had not worked out as he had planned, sorry that Grandad had refused to become debloated, refused to come back and be Grandad again. He put his hand on her cheek to wipe away the tears, to touch her, to comfort her, but Mam jerked away from him, her eyes glinting strangely as though he had attacked her. Don't you touch me, she snapped. Don't you dare touch me!

Sorry Mam, said Pericles, lost.

Pericles dries his feet in the grass, then stands and does a little jig to warm himself and get the stiffness from his bones. He likes the night time best of all. The scuffles and skitterings in the reeds and rushes are the friendliest things he can imagine. It is the day which seems to reveal all that is harsh and unfriendly. Harshness rattles through his mind: the fox decapitated, the chickens throatless, Grandad bursting at the seams. Sadness sweeps over him as he thinks again of the terrible fate of the little fox: the frightened animal's dependence on him had pleased him and made him feel needed.

Now, who's going to help me? asked Miss Hudson.

Help, shouted Grandad.

Help squawked the chickens.

Help, yelped the fox.

Help.

Got the dirty thievin' bastard, said Grandad triumphantly; and Pericles remembered this and repeated it as he dug his knife deep into the bloated corpse: Got the dirty thievin' bastard.

The old man's eyelids shook and Pericles knew Grandad was watching him. Thievin' bastard, he shouted again.

Put it *here*, Poppy told him knowingly: but that had been sometime later.

Suddenly Pericles has a great yearning to visit the woods and he sets off in that direction, jogging along the river bank. An old owl zooms out of the dark slicing the night like a skiff cutting through a calm sea, its wings rustling the few remaining dead leaves which cling tenaciously to an old beech. That is the only sound in the wood, the brittle whisper of those dead leaves, as Pericles creeps along, quiet as an Indian brave, careful to do nothing that might disrupt the heavy peacefulness. He is fastidious, too, about where he places his feet, avoiding the flowers. He feels a warm cloak of contentment wrap itself about him the further he penetrates.

Come on, Pericles. Let's go into the woods, said Poppy Burn, her eyes shining excitedly. Winter had been kind to her and she had developed a lot in the last few months.

Pericles shook his head.

Aw, come on. I know a great place.

Again he shook his head, looking slightly annoyed now.

Why not? You afraid of the dark or something?

No.

I think you are! Hell, you don't have to be frightened. I've been there lots of times in the dark, Poppy told him. With boys, she added significantly.

If she had expected Pericles to be interested, or perhaps jealous, she was unlucky. The woods, he knew quite well, only came into existence when he was present in them: as soon as he withdrew they vanished, vanished like the fox, invisible like the old owl, became as invisible as he did himself at times.

– and we had a right good time, Poppy Burn was saying.

Good, said Pericles generously.

But I think you'd be better. I'd be better with you, anyway.

When I'm ready I'll take you to the woods. *I'll* show you the woods properly, Pericles told her kindly.

When *you're* ready! Poppy bridled.

Yes.

You're not *that* bloody great, you know. I don't think I even want you now, Poppy told him haughtily, but she was interested all the same.

It was from that day, although some instinct told him it had nothing whatever to do with Poppy Burn, that Pericles started to get his woods ready and in order.

Silently now, he moves along the river bank, leaping from bank to bank at intervals as though to obliterate his tracks, yet each crossing some vital thread in a meticulously woven scheme.

Like some bloody animal, he is, Dad complained. The way he can creep about and hide himself!

He's just a child playing, Mam explained.

Some child, Dad snorted.

Don't be at him, Mam told Dad. The way you and Big Mike bully him is it any wonder the boy is addled.

I don't bully him, woman, Dad gaped, mystified by the accusation.

Yes you do. You're for ever shouting at him and calling him names.

He never even hears anything he doesn't want to. Sly as a snake, that's what he is.

You see? There you are at it again.

Well he *is* like a snake, Dad said defensively. You just watch him sometime when he doesn't know you're looking. He can vanish right before your eyes. I've seen him do it hundreds of times.

Oh, for heaven's sake, Bill. Vanish, indeed. He just likes to play games. You keep making him sound – well, evil.

That's just what he is, Dad agreed. Evil. And dangerous.

Don't be ridiculous. Evil and dangerous!

– not dangerous, said the doctor, but he will need care and

great patience.

Depart Satan! Father Denis Redmond, his spirits bolstered by one pre-ceremonial drink, suitably attired for the occasion, felt conspicuously embarrassed by the farcical situation as he towered over the kneeling boy like some demented witch-doctor trying to raise a juvenile Lazarus. It was as though he was guilty of trying to banish forever some familiar from his life. Not that this particular acquaintance showed the remotest sign of packing his bag and moving on, not even, it became evident, of donning his hat and coat and going for a quiet stroll in the garden as he, Father Redmond, had done six months or six years ago with his friend Matthew Warren, bishop of the church of Rome.

A stroll in the garden and a cup of tea – or even a romp with Beatrix Potter cures most things, the Bishop replied mysteriously to Father Redmond's: Jesus, Matthew, I'm sorry. I can't help bouncing about. They call it the heebie-jeebies, don't they? It's like trying to stand upright on a clap of thunder!

That would be a neat trick, Denis.

Standing upright, you mean? I see. Yes. Yes it is. But on the other hand, on manus otherus you might say, there is something quite inordinately amicable about the wildness, don't you think?

I wouldn't really know –

Why doom and damnation should always be orchestrated by celestial symphonic rumblings is beyond me.

Speaking of doom –

Ah –

– tell me, Denis, what *are* we going to do with you?

Do you know, Matthew, Father Redmond asked suddenly, that people used to leave their doors open during thunderstorms so that Jesus could stroll in and shelter from the inclemency?

I know – they still do in Mexico, I understand, but I suspect you already know that.

The trouble is, what *else* might take advantage of such hospitality? Ah, now *there's* the rubadubdub. Like keeping an open mind. Fatal. Quite suicidal. All *that* ever does is allow the unprecedented free admission as if one didn't have enough trouble dealing with the thunderbolt that falls on oneself –

Could we leave the atmospheric intrusions for a moment, Denis? You and I simply have to try and work this thing out –

I could use a drink, Matthew –

Denis, for the love of God –

Indeed, Father Redmond agreed willingly. You might just have put your bejewelled episcopal finger on it, Matthew. I have all the love in the world for God, but He insists on avoiding me.

I'm tempted to say I don't altogether blame Him, the Bishop confided, smiling thinly. Denis, we've decided to ask you – mind the steps here, they're a bit tricky, the aubretia having got the better of its argument with the stone, hee, hee – to go to –

I remember I was in a church once – I'm sorry to interrupt you but I'm sure you'll find this interesting – it must be quite a while ago, trying to pray, trying, you might say, to grab a spot of that love you were talking about before the market was cornered, so to speak, and I heard an extraordinary thing. Shall I tell you, Matthew, what I heard?

I can hardly control my excitement, the Bishop said patiently.

I actually heard a woman in the confessional tell the priest to go to hell! Can you imagine that? It was the funniest thing I had ever heard.

Hmmm. I can't see why.

She should have come to me, of course.

Of course –

– but then she could hardly have known I've spent the last God alone knows how long there, could she? In hell. Christ, Matthew, I really do need a drink.

Denis, we've decided to give you one last chance – we've

decided to send you to a small parish on the –

The trouble is, as I see it – and I still do see some things quite clearly, you know – the trouble is it is so damnably hard to stick to the law of the church and be compassionate at the same time. A small parish– Oh, I think not. I'm quite happy where –

We have decided, Denis. It will only –

Blake found a path through hell, did you know that?

Denis! Will you stop chattering for *one* minute –

– forbidden to all but himself, of course, which was a bit niggardly, you must admit, but I do see it signposted from time to time in my dreams.

The bishop stopped suddenly, placing himself in front of Father Redmond and blocking his path. For heaven's sake will you listen to me, Denis –

I *am* listening to you, Matthew. What is this parochial parish you and your fellow dignitaries have located for me? Not that I need to be moved, I'm really much better than I was last year, Father Redmond lied hopefully.

I wish you'd try and understand that we're only trying to help you. We're only thinking of you. Anything we decide is for your own good.

Very droll, Matthew. Ah, dear, do you know how many atrocities have been performed in the name of that phrase? What you really mean is that it's for *your* good, don't you?

You'll insist on looking at it like that no matter what I say. In any case it's academic.

Never mind. When do you want me to go?

We thought September. I really am sorry, Denis. I know you're not responsible for most of the absurd things you do but last week's episode scandalized too many people.

And that was undoubtedly true. Even Denis Redmond could understand this although he could also see that, once again, he had been grossly misunderstood. He turned from the tabernacle and made his way carefully down the carpeted steps to the altar rails (the ciborium filled with Hosts which he himself had transformed into the body of Christ, that same Christ for Whom he had all the love in the world but Who rejected him out of hand). He could have warned them, but changed his mind. Who would have believed him? Who would have stayed to listen if he had suddenly announced, My dear brethren something out of the ordinary is about to take place? He stared out long and hard at the congregation. There, heads bowed with reverence and indomitable faith, was the inevitable multitude of Sunday worshippers. The entire building echoed with the excited, sensual hum he had noticed so often as people muttered their belated adorations, cleansing their souls to receive holy communion. Their faith was so uncomplicated, it was as though the Christ they were about to accept was a different Christ from the one he had given to himself moments before: theirs was the Christ of love and compassion and understanding, and he had an overwhelming, uncontrollable desire to share this. Suddenly, horribly, he was sitting on the bottom step of the altar, the ciborium viced between his knees, while with both hands he was thrusting the sacred hosts into his mouth, chewing and swallowing compulsively, slobbering and shaking beyond control.

Yes, I'm sorry about that, Matthew. I don't quite know what came over me. At least I do. I was trying to share in – never mind. I suppose you had them banging on the palace door?

You could say that. Politely, of course.

Of course.

A bit of purple can be very off-putting, the Bishop smiled.

Indeed. How ever did you explain it to them?

I didn't. I just asked them to pray for you.

Ah.

As you know we all pray for you, Denis.

Yes, do that. Thank you, Matthew.

We'll pray for you, Father, the woman said. She smiled at Dad: he's a good priest, she said as they watched Father Redmond walk unsteadily from the farmyard. It was frightening that bit about 'depart Satan' though, wasn't it?

Made bugger all difference if you ask me, Dad said. For God's sake tell the fool to get up off his knees.

Don't be so cranky with him, Mam said. It must all be a terrible shock to him.

Not half the shock he'll get from me if he doesn't watch out from now on.

Pericles comes at last to his destination: a small island created by the unexpectedly frivolous meanderings of the river. A marvellous old willow grows in the centre and cuddles the island to its roots making a protective canopy over it. Under the hanging boughs the earth has been stamped with bare feet leaving it compact and almost smooth: only the small indentations of toes are clear but they decorate it nicely. Three huge boulders are arranged in one corner, boulders which Pericles himself has hauled from the disused quarry two miles away, always at night so as not to be noticed. It was gruelling work and he is still not altogether sure why he needs them but something insists they are essential to an overall plan. One rock was so large and cumbersome that he had been worn out when only half way back from the quarry, so he had rolled it into a ditch and covered it with moss and leaves and come back for it the next night. This rock, an almost perfect rectangle, formed the centrepiece of his arrangement. He had chipped away at it over a long period so that it seemed to shine even in the gloom, and when the sunlight filtered through the willow it sparkled and looked very pretty. And on this rock, perhaps carefully placed, or perhaps just left there for the moment, is his hunting knife.

One good thing, Dad said, that bloody murderous knife is gone once and for all.

Pericles smiled quietly.

Pericles smiles quietly as he looks about him. Certainly as far as he is concerned there is nothing magical or sinister or portentous in the setting.

Poor fox. Get up, damn you.

Where's that knife of yours, Grandad wanted to know.

Damn fool, Dad said.

He puts things away and then forgets where they are, Mam explained reasonably.

Needs to be put away himself, Dad muttered.

Don't, Mam pleaded.

Unfortunately Pericles had forgotten that the knife was supposed to be gone for good and all, and he practised throwing it in the manner Grandad had described. Amazingly the knife seemed to take on a spirit of its own and flew further and further away, landing with a thud near one of the workmen in the cornfield, and the game was up.

Now look, Mr Stort, the workman said with a deference which pleased Dad, I know you've got your troubles like I've got mine but –

Where's that knife, Dad wanted to know immediately.

Pericles screwed up his face and shrugged.

Alas, once again he had forgotten and tried to reincarnate Grandad and they all knew that he still had the knife and were a little more afraid of him. For many days he had left the old man's blood (if that was what the strange discoloured liquid was called) on the knife, liking the design it made when dry, and the sense of utility it gave the steel. But when they heaved the corpse into the hearse and took it away, the blood was connected with nothing in the boy's mind so he cleaned it off, and polished and honed and oiled the knife nicely. Then he placed it on the granite block for the first time.

Pericles lopes about his retreat. Soon, he thinks, it will be ready. He must simply wait now: nothing more, just wait. Whatever else is needed will be provided, whatever else remains to be done will be done. It will be done of itself or aided by some force the name of which Pericles does not know; but he knows it exists or will exist and then everything will be in order. God will provide, said Grandma; and it would be from some deity of his own that Pericles would receive assistance.

The devil provides a lot quicker, said Big Mike who knew everything, scoffing.

We'll get on famously, said someone.

Pericles leaves the island and makes his secret way back through the woods towards home. Suddenly, without questioning his reason for doing so, he reels away from the path that leads to the farmhouse and heads, instead, for a mysterious square of light he can just make out near the schoolhouse. He feels suddenly very cold, and he shivers, shaking himself in a curious downward movement like a horse, but he feels inexplicably excited at the same time as though on the brink of solving many riddles. His instinct warns him to be quiet and stealthy so he creeps a little closer quietly and stealthily. He slows his pace even more a hundred yards from the light and then, dropping on all fours, he crawls towards the lighted window, scrupulously avoiding the radiance thrown on the ground –

Let there be light said God, said Miss Hudson, and there was light.

Pericles wrote it down legibly.

Put the light out first, Mam said, concerned. The children might be awake and look in.

Think they don't know? growled Dad already on top of her. Known all their lives.

Of course they don't. They're only children, Mam sighed.

Haw. How long are you going to go on keeping them as children in your mind, woman.

That's all they are.

Like as not doing it themselves half the time, Dad grunted, grinding himself into position.

I wish you wouldn't talk like that, Bill.

Dad was already heaving so he didn't answer her.

Feel this, said Big Mike, and blocked out the light with the blanket by pulling it over his head.

Tricia Hudson takes off her stockings, blows into them sharply, and hangs them with exaggerated care on the special bar at the end of her bed. She moves happily about her room singing brief snatches of Hark, Hark, the Lark quietly to herself in a somewhat mutilated soprano as she prepares for bed. Finally, she comes to rest in front of the full-length mirror on the inside of the wardrobe door, and primps: why, yes, she admits to herself, she still has a very seductive body – appetising the artificial kiwi had called it! I could eat you, he told her hungrily, eagerly stripping off his ridiculous stars-and-stripes underpants and joining her in bed with a tremendous leap. The trouble was, when he had finished his meal and hygienically set sail for the bathroom, Tricia Hudson felt uneasily mortified by the inadequacy of it all. Worse still, five minutes later (while he snorted and gargled and spewed water like some demented ocean mammal), she felt as though nothing whatever had taken place, as though the only significant thing was a short, sharp deflowering pain. And when he returned to the bedroom, whistling as unconcernedly as any genial genital hit-man, even taking a small bow as though anticipating an ovation for his performance (if, indeed, a rather sloppy gluttonous gorging could be called a performance), she was already sitting up in bed, her nightdress draped about her shoulders showing her summer tan merging into the whiteness of her breasts, both hands turned palm upwards in an involuntary gesture of appeal, epitomising her incommunicable longing to have someone very special of her own to love. And as she watched him dress with brilliant well-practised rapidity, and the air of a job well done, vague images of grief and tragedy and loneliness flickered in her mind. He had, it was true, kissed her lightly on the cheek before he left, vowing he would be waiting impatiently for their next encounter which would be next Wednesday (all right?) in the Vine and Grapes (all right?) between seven thirty and eight (all right?).

Tricia Hudson brushes her hair vigorously, pressing the hard

79

bristles fiercely into her scalp.

Always *brush* your hair, someone told her. Only brushing will make it shine like it should.

Yes, I will. I'll remember that.

Vigy, for the love of heaven will get you upstairs this minute and comb those dreadful tangles out of your hair, Mam wailed. You look like a scarecrow.

Aw, Mam, I'm not going nowhere. Nobody will see me.

I can see you. Upstairs this instant.

Alone, Mam ran her fingers through her own coarse and thinning hair and bridled contentedly as Patrick Bullock ran his fingers through her soft and flowing red hair.

You'll wait for me, Eileen?

You won't come back. You'll fall in love in the city.

Oh, no. I'll be back for you.

Patrick, Patrick, do you think I don't know. I've seen all the young men go and never a one return.

You can come to me in the city, then –

Mam shook her head: You know I belong here, she said. Let us just enjoy each other while you *are* here.

I love you, Eileen.

And I love you.

Well, then –

Shhh.

Shhh, scolded Mam as Big Mike thumped into the kitchen. I've just got the baby to sleep.

Her hair brushed and shining and tied back from her face with a band of white ribbon Tricia Hudson removes her brassiere: her neat little breasts topple forward and stand up perkily with a small pool of blood floating on the top of each.

Vigy tugged off the old bra she had borrowed from Mam and her enormous breasts sagged like a Kikuyu's. She hated them, but she knew the boys didn't.

Pericles watches Miss Hudson thinking it would be nice if he could persuade her to do all this again knowing he was watching. He shifts from one foot to the other, not even blinking, his lips moist and slightly apart. Miss Hudson is talking to her reflection in the mirror: telling herself a story perhaps.

You are a damn fool Tricia Hudson, Tricia Hudson tells herself with restrained affection.

You *are* a fool, Tricia dear, someone told her in that expansive voice of someone who had been through it all, but not unkindly.

I know, replied Tricia, and laughed a tight nervous titter.

Why on earth didn't you do something about it?

Like what?

Good God, we're out of the Dark Ages, you know. There are ways of –

Abortion?

Yes.

I thought about it. But – don't you dare laugh – I kept hoping it would go away.

Like a headache, I suppose? Really, you're impossible.

I suppose I am.

Well, what are you going to do *now*?

– ? Why, have the baby, of course.

But you *can't*!

Whyever not?

You know why.

Women do it all the time –

I know they do, stupid. But you're not married –

What happened to those Dark Ages all of a sudden?

This is different.

I don't see how.

People will forgive you for making a mistake if you have the good sense to get rid of it. But if you have it without being married they'll think you're not only stupid but immoral. They'll think you're flaunting it.

It's pretty academic anyway, isn't it, since it's far too late to do anything but have the child – and, by the way, I wish you wouldn't keep referring to my unborn child as 'it'.

'It' seems easier. No offence meant. Why don't you get whoever it was to marry you?

No, thank you very much.

He can't be that dreadful if you went to bed with him in the first place. I mean if he got *you* into bed he must be pretty terrific.

Ha. I never said he was dreadful. He wasn't in fact. Actually, I think I used him more than the other way around.

But *you've* landed up with the bundle – sorry, child.

True.

Well, if you won't do the obvious, and you won't get married, I presume you'll at least have the wit to have the child adopted.

I haven't decided yet.

But you *must*.

It depends how I feel afterwards.

All you'll feel is damn sore and not a damn thing you can do about it. I know.

You're cynical.

With reason, I can tell you. And you will be too before long if you don't try and be sensible.

I can't make any decision at the moment. I've got to wait and see. We're not exactly talking about dirty washing, are we?

All *I* know is that I hope *you* know what you're doing.

I don't yet. But I will.

Knowing you you'll get all sentimental and want to keep it –

We'll see.

And as she lay in the maternity ward after her child's delivery she was amazed and rather shocked that her feelings then were almost identical to those she experienced on the evening of her son's conception: as though nothing of any import had taken place. And it was precisely this vacant numbness which consoled her when she waved away her right to the infant, for how, she tried to rationalize, how could she love the tiny creature conceived and born with such a pittance of affection?

You are quite, quite certain that this is what you want, the doctor who formed his words with vowels of disapproval asked her again.

Yes, doctor. I'm quite sure.

You have given it enough thought?

Quite enough.

You've spoken to the father?

He wouldn't be interested.

Not interested in his own son?

He doesn't believe the child is his.

Ah.

Tricia fixed her eyes on the disapproving face. It *is* his, though, she said.

I see. Well, if you've definitely made up your mind –

I have. Please don't prolong things.

I just hope you don't live to regret it. I hate adoptions personally. They never allow the dust to settle. Memory always blows back into one's eyes, he told her enigmatically. I mean physically the child can be handed on, but spiritually it – he, in your case – has a habit of staying around one for ever.

For God's sake –

I'm sorry. I shouldn't have –

No you shouldn't. I told you what I wanted.

Very well. I'll take care of everything.

Miss Hudson takes her sky-blue nightdress from the wardrobe and arranges it prettily on the bed. She turns down the covers and smoothes the pillow after patting it affectionately as she might a friendly terrier. She sets the alarm on her bedside travelling clock, letting it ring shrilly for a few seconds to make sure it still functions.

The clock on the wall had something written on it but it did not ring shrilly. Fettered bird fluffing feathers in timebath.

Don't you back chat the teacher or I'll have your hide for harness.

83

Beautiful Pericles.

Vigy lay naked on her bed, panting sighs as deep as orgasms, watched over by her private lovers – an astonishing conglomeration of posters, portraying sulky young men in various attitudes and most in advanced stages of acne, which festooned the wall over her bed.

Get into bed and cover yourself, you randy bitch, warned Big Mike, only half hoping to be obeyed.

It's too hot, replied Vigy, fanning her breasts with a magazine.

You're too hot, said Big Mike hoarsely.

Huh, grunted Vigy.

Never mind your huh, said Big Mike. I know damn well what you're after.

Vigy stretched luxuriously as a cat.

Feel this, said Big Mike, but not to Pericles.

You can't do much anyway, Vigy taunted her brother. You're my brother.

So's Pericles, said Big Mike ominously.

What's that supposed to mean, demanded Vigy urgently, sitting up and consigning the magazine to the darkness under her bed.

I saw you both at it in the barn.

I don't care what you saw. Anyway, he's not really my brother. Mam and Dad only took him in, didn't they?

Shut up!

The barn was still damp from the winter rain and the lower bales of hay had started to smell rancid. Pericles, come and give me a hand, will you? called Vigy. Field mice skittered about the floor in dozens since the old barn cat, long since outnumbered and outwitted, had retreated to the rafters and washed itself continuously in lofty isolation. Come up here on top of the hay and I'll show you what I want you to do, called Vigy breathlessly. Pericles liked it high up in the hay with Vigy who was sweating and had her blouse open all the way down the front.

84

I saw you all right, said Big Mike, and don't you think I didn't.

Pericles opened Miss Hudson's closed button for her kindly.

Good boys always ask first.

Yes, ma'am.

Now, where shall we sit?

Christ! exclaimed Vigy, humping these bales is no work for me. Here, rub my back, will you?

Pericles rubbed his sister's back. Lower, said Vigy softly. And Pericles rubbed lower.

I saw you, said Big Mike who knew everything.

You're *always* gawking, Vigy told him. That's about all you ever do – gawk.

Tricia Hudson selects a book from her portable library of what she likes to call her 'good' books: *A Guide for the Bedevilled*, by Ben Hecht. Pericles wonders if this is the book the teacher reads from at school. Without opening it Tricia Hudson abruptly changes her mind, choosing instead William James's *Varieties of Religious Experience* and opening it at random. For a few minutes she sits lost in thought, staring at the printed words which seem to have the power of carrying her mind back through the years to her father demanding practical information about becoming a magician of either hue. Poor William James would have been of small help there! The key to the matter, her father explained to her, the key was to induce a satisfactory copulation between the subnormal world and the abnormally suspicious – whatever he meant by that. Mildly shaken, Tricia Hudson closes the book sharply and throws it across the bed away from her. Watching, Pericles is curiously upset that she has not read to him. She must have forgotten. Furtively he taps on the window: toc.

Miss Hudson added many stars and planets to her wonderful firmament: toc, toc.

I saw you, droned Big Mike monotonously.

Gosh, I'm *tired*, moaned Vigy and collapsed exotically into

85

the hay. Her skirt rose high on her thighs and Pericles saw a little bunch of hair as though small furry animals had requisitioned her legtops as hiding places. Aren't you tired too, Pericles, Vigy suggested. He wasn't particularly but he was in a good humour so he lay down beside her anyway.

Tricia Hudson glances at the window uncertainly and makes to move towards it. Then she shakes her head and smiles to herself and jumps into bed joined by the strident voice of Delia Murphy who sings, 'Tis the ivy, dear mother, against the glass tapping' in her mind.

Pericles taps on the window again, louder.

I saw you, Big Mike droned on endlessly.

What's that supposed to mean anyway, asked Vigy wriggling her toes and wishing that one of her pin-ups would suddenly materialize and crush his weight on to her.

Big Mike pushed himself up on to one elbow and leered across the room at her. He had great cords running down his arms which were covered by a fine reddish fur. You want me to come over and tell you? he asked; and Pericles could feel his brother's body start to quiver.

Put to it Vigy hesitated, but only for a moment. All right, she said casually enough: it could be fun to try Big Mike, who was supposed to know what he was doing.

Pericles watched them with his normal curiosity: the intimacy of their act meant little to him really, but he studied them carefully nonetheless since everything Big Mike did was of some importance and could prove useful later.

Tricia Hudson very slowly pulls back the blankets and gets out of bed. She tiptoes to the window and, making blinkers of her hands, peers out but does not immediately see the boy hidden in the shadows. Pericles remains motionless.

We'll get on famously.

No, Bill. Not again, Mam pleaded.

But Vigy did not say no to Big Mike and he stayed with her on her bed for many hours; sometimes they lay still, sometimes they moved in joint contortions.

And Pericles watched.

Big Mike, could I do what you did with Vigy last night?

Naw, replied Big Mike, suddenly alarmed.

Why not?

You couldn't, that's all.

Are you sure?

I'm sure. Shut up.

But Pericles tried anyway and found that he could.

Vigy rolled towards him in the hay, clambering on top of him. He was agreeably surprised: he had never known Vigy do this to him before and he enjoyed the intimacy of her body. She dangled her breasts in his face as she pushed herself up on her hands. Small pools of blood capped them and Pericles cleaned them for her with his tongue.

Hmmm, groaned Vigy.

Wow, said Poppy Burn.

Beautiful, said Miss Hudson.

Wow, said Vigy.

Hmm, said Miss Hudson.

Tricia Hudson shakes her head irritably and frowns. Even through the flimsy sky-blue nightdress Pericles can see her caps of blood.

Can I do that. Naw.

If Dad finds out he'll murder us both for sure, Vigy said giggling.

He won't ever know, Big Mike assured her, heaving urgently.

There's him, Vigy said, trying to nod her head towards Pericles.

He doesn't know what we're doing.

But he's watching.

Let him watch. Damn fool.

I don't like being watched. Not like that. It's creepy.

Creepy, shit. I want another go.

Hmm, agreed Vigy, only not so rough. I'm getting sore.

You must be out of practice.

That's one thing I'm not.

Shut up.

Pericles watched Big Mike's body heave up and down on his sister and noted the glaze of satisfaction on Vigy's face. She liked it well enough.

You keep well clear of that Poppy Burn, Dad warned him severely.

He won't go near her, Mam said. He's not that sort.

Maybe not, Dad almost agreed. But that bitch will be after him, you can be sure of that.

Oh, she's not that bad, Mam said.

Not that bad? Not that bad? Dad always repeated things when he got really angry. Christ, she'd teach a donkey how to do it if she could find one stupid enough to go with her.

Bill! Mam said, shocked.

You can believe me, Dad told her.

You can believe me, Patrick Bullock told her. I'll be back for you.

Maybe sometime – but not in time, Mam told him not quite sure why she had chosen those words.

Pericles taps on the window again: he drums his nails on the pane and the clock clops in his head. Toc, toc, toc.

Tricia Hudson jumps out of bed again irritably.

If Dad finds out he'll murder the both of us for sure.

Let's do it again, said Big Mike.

Wow, said Poppy Burn, where *did* you learn to do it like that?

Pericles uncoils himself from the shadows and smiles a beaming smile at the teacher.

'Pericles Stort! What on earth are you doing here at this time of night?'

'Just looking, ma'am.'

'Looking?'

She's a proper lady and you call her ma'am if you have to talk to her, Mam warned him patiently.

'That's right, ma'am,' says Pericles politely.

'At what for heaven's sake?'

I've been looking for you everywhere, chook, the genital hit-man told her.

Really.

Yes. Really. I told you I wanted to see you again. I was very, very upset.

Poor you. I can just imagine.

You forgot our date, didn't you?

I was there.

Oh.

Yes. Oh.

I got all tied up. I did try to get there, though. Honest injun.

I'm sure you did.

Hell, what's the matter, chook – we had a good time didn't we?

Not from my point of view – and for God's sake stop calling me chook.

I'm sorry. I only –

Forget it. It's my fault. What is this 'chook' anyway?

Ah. Well, that's what New Zealanders call a chicken –

Thanks a lot!

What's got into you anyway? You're so uptight.

I happen to be pregnant –

Pregnant!

Yes. Pregnant. Hello Daddy.

Jesus! It's not mine, is it?

Well, it's not a virgin birth if that's what you're hoping.

Oh, God. You're sure it's mine?

The baby is yours.

How can you know – for certain, I mean. I can't have been the only one –

You bastard. You know damn well you were the only one I

89

let near me.

You're joking –

I'm not, you know.

Jesus God. You'll have to do something about it quick – get rid of it somehow.

And what would you suggest – chook! – flush it down the loo?

I didn't mean –

Oh, go away. You make me sick.

But –

You needn't lose any sleep over it. I have no intention of involving you in any way.

You mean that?

I mean it. You're not worth the trouble.

That's a –

Anyway, I'd like my child to have a *man* for a father, not some cheap hit-and-run predator.

Look, if you need anything –

I don't.

Sure?

Certain. I did, though. I needed you badly – never mind. You wouldn't understand.

'Oh . . . at you, ma'am,' explains Pericles.

Not in a million years would you understand.

Christ, I just thought you wanted a good time –

Even that you couldn't give me.

I thought I did.

Why should you have thought that? Just because you grunted and groaned and heaved and satisfied yourself? Oh, go away. Just go away and let me be.

'At me? Why should you want to look at me, Pericles?' Tricia Hudson asks nervously, unsure what she is letting herself in for.

'Just because,' says Pericles. The teacher smells of babysoap even at night.

Wow, said Poppy. You're even better than Big Mike. He just grunts, but *you*.

Pericles watched Big Mike seduce Vigy and noted each tortuous move and tucked them away in that area of his mind given over to retaining postures and sighs. Later he transferred them to a more private cell and practised: his enthusiasm created ingenious variations as his gentle brain made love to straining, sensuous images.

'Just because,' he tells the teacher again.

'That's hardly a reason, Pericles,' says Miss Hudson. 'Just because is not a reason, is it?'

Pericles resorts to his hitherto successful bashful smile of encouragement and reaches out tentatively to touch her. As Miss Hudson steps back in automatic alarm the boy's finger becomes hooked in the V of her nightdress and the delicate material rips to the waist. Two perky white breasts show pools of blood above the white belly, a round white belly with a strange demarcation as though someone had used a knife and made an incision and then stuck the flesh together again.

Tricia Hudson slaps the boy in the face as hard as she can, and Pericles stops smiling, puzzled.

We'll get on famously, beautiful Pericles.

Let's go into the woods, said Poppy.

Somewhere else, insisted Pericles.

Where?

By the river. In the reeds.

Okay.

Pericles pressed Poppy down into the reeds, ignoring her unexpected pleas that Jesus! she was getting soaked. Poppy struggled furiously and, to his surprise, Pericles found he rather liked that. She hit him about the head with fists as hard as a man's. Her legs lashed out kicking the air, and she even attempted to bite him, but Pericles was not to be put off: he had her skirt raised high and rubbed his hand back and forth over her round belly as white as the inside of a fox's pelt and fingered the little scar as though someone before him had used a knife and made a slit and stuck the flesh together again.

You – you damn savage, Poppy shouted at him. I didn't mean you to *do* anything. Christ, you just wait 'till I tell your Dad.

You keep well away from that Poppy Burn, Dad warned.

You've only gone and broken me, Poppy sobbed. That's what you've done, and me with no protection.

Sorry, said Pericles, but he had absolutely no idea for what he was apologizing.

'Sorry, ma'am,' says Pericles softly.

You're a bloody rapist, screamed Poppy as Pericles eased himself out of her, quietly amazed at all that had taken place.

'Oh, my God!' exclaims Miss Hudson, hugging herself tightly.

Poppy, said Pericles gently.

'Ma'am,' says Pericles gently.

Look at me. Just you look at me, Poppy Burn wept. Wringing wet and pregnant too, she added, as though unable to make up her mind which calamity was the worse.

'I'm sure it was an accident,' Miss Hudson is saying, deciding placation is the wisest course to take under the circumstances. 'And I shouldn't have hit you. I'm sorry.'

'Yes, ma'am,' agrees Pericles agreeably.

Poppy Burn lunged to her feet and fled across the field looking grotesque as she tried to raise her knickers and lower her skirt at the same time.

'I think you'd better be off home now,' suggests Miss Hudson hopefully. 'I'm sure your parents will be worried about you. We'll just forget what happened, shall we?'

'Yes, ma'am.'

'Goodnight, then,' the teacher says firmly and closes the window awkwardly with one hand.

An owl screams not too far away; it continues to scream from time to time as it glides through the night, moving farther and farther afield. With its passing a strange and eerie silence falls over the boy's world: it is as though the owl has warned every living thing of dreadful things to come, warned them to be silent and to watch. The light in the teacher's room goes out and Pericles finds himself blinking in the darkness, dazzled by the flecks of light which linger in his eyes, and he notices for the first time that his face stings sorely.

Whatever have you done to your face? Mam wanted to know. It's all red on one side.

Damn fool, muttered Dad.

Don't always pick on the boy, Mam whined, and she treated him with a special smothering kindness for a few days. He picked her purse from the floor of the train that took them to the ferry and freed her shoulders of loose hair.

I'm going straight to tell your Dad, Poppy turned and yelled when she knew she was out of reach, but the threat seemed small and useless as it bounced across the grass and reached him in a whisper.

Dad will bloody murder the both of us if he finds out, said Vigy.

No he won't, insisted Big Mike.

Pericles watched Vigy and Big Mike on the bed, and he rollicked with marvellous Miss Hudson who smelled of baby-soap

It starts to rain gently before Pericles decides to move on. He feels his jaw and smiles to himself. He takes one final look through the window and sees the shape near the window move away, gliding like a fish in deep water.

Got one, said Grandad triumphantly. And then he slipped.

Tricia Hudson stands back from the window, still hugging herself, rocking gently, consoling someone who for all she can tell is not herself. Strangely, she is not frightened. In the warm maternal embrace within which she consoles herself there seems to be a corner set aside for the pathetic yet disquietingly lovable child she has just struck. It is as though his yearning

93

spirit (that heart-rending yearning she herself can so well recognize) lies in the cradle of her arms and nudges gently but continually for what she can only think of as the milk of human protection. But look here, all things considered, I have a perfect right to be here nuzzling your breast, the longing seems to be saying to her reasonably, settling one nipple firmly between its lips. You misunderstand me totally If you think I have merely gatecrashed my way into your life since you must be fully aware that I have never left it and, indeed, if you insist on thinking otherwise how can I convince you that it is so? But I do beg you to look at me carefully. Then, perhaps, you will find your answer. See – see how alike we are we two, how we seem to be one: what beauty can compare with the unifying bond that exists between mother and –

Tricia Hudson slumps on her bed, trembling violently.

– but that would require the talent of a great artist. If only I could paint, her father sighed, which seemed an odd sort of thing for a man on the point of expiring to long for.

You can always take it up when you come home, Tricia told him kindly, taking his bony hand in hers and tickling the palm delicately as though signalling some secret Italian love contract. Even in death, it struck her remorselessly, her father was something of a clown, referring to his imminent departure as 'Isis calling from the potting shed' while at the same time taking out some class of death insurance by confessing his sins obliquely to the resident Franciscan.

He rolled his head on the crisp white hospital pillow-case: We both know I won't be home again. There is no need for *us* to pretend, is there?

Tricia felt the tears well up in her eyes.

Don't think I *mind* dying, her father went on, squeezing her hand affectionately. I know exactly where I'm going. I've been there so often, you see. It's very pleasant. Filled with old friends. I'll be perfectly happy I assure you. The only thing that does trouble me a little is that I have no image of Sefer to take with me. Not even the vaguest impression. That is quite strange –

Don't be silly. Of course you'll be home soon. And I'm not pretending either.

Her father glanced at her sideways and raised an eyebrow quizzically. Why is everyone so hellbent on keeping me alive, I wonder, he asked sadly.

Why? Because we love you, of course. Why else?

I see. I see. Strange, I've always thought if we really loved our friends – and we are friends, aren't we, Tricia? – if we *really* loved our friends we would let them die when they wanted to and not plug them into this horrific gadgetry until *we* decide the time is ripe. That would be much kinder, don't you think? After all, we only force them to take out an unredeemable mortgage on their soul – and you will recall what happened to a certain gentleman who tried *that* particular remedy?

Tricia smiled wanly at her father: I'm sorry. I didn't really understand, did I?

Don't worry child. We never do – more often than not we never even try to. You know the oddest thing about dying?

Tricia Hudson shook her head.

Shall I tell you? her father asked, his voice already croaking with death. It is the astonishing warm silence. It is as though the most benevolent of the gods has reached down and lowered the volume to allow your mind to concentrate on the glorious peace that lies ahead. Ah, how kind. How generous. How very considerate.

Hush, Tricia whispered. Hush.

He looked at her for a long time, screwing up his eyes as though finding some difficulty in bringing her into focus; or perhaps he was seeing something he had never seen before, something which would not quite reveal its identity, and he was puzzled by its anonymity. What he said next was always to remain a mystery for the words kept blurring and dissembling. What it sounded like was 'My soul is like the driest dust being blown over the fertile land of colourful zinnias,' but her father would surely never have said such a thing. Or maybe he would, for by that time he had no need to comprehend anything of the words beyond their abject confirmation that he was dead. It was hard for Tricia to believe that life had gone from his body since his eyes were still so bright: the deathly glaze she had expected failed to cloud them. Worse, they were not contented eyes. They looked hurt and disappointed as though in the final moments of his life he had been let down, almost as though some friend of long standing had failed to keep the appointment.

Pericles hunches his shoulders, shoves his hands in his pockets, and sets off across the fields for home. Far away a ship gives a foggy blast and Pericles sees himself in the railway carriage again looking out of the window with its small red sticker proclaiming that smoking is not allowed. It is very dark outside although the sun appears to be shining and Miss Hudson is out there in the darkness moving along beside him at the same pace but in her own private shadowy carriage. The ticket collector takes the stubs and smiles and says thank you sonny and Mam smiles and says thank you son. And thank you Pericles said Miss Hudson when he finished cleaning off her breasts with his tongue.

As soon as he reaches the house Pericles takes off his boots and leaves them by the warm stove in the kitchen. He creeps up the stairs, missing the fifth and ninth which creak and wake Dad who yells at him: Damn fool what's he been up to at this time of night. But the house is quiet as a grave as he undresses and folds his clothes with great precision, placing each garment one on top of the other, making a neat and tidy pile on the old wooden chest at the end of the bed he shares with Big Mike who knows everything and who now grinds his teeth like a horse chomping its bit and rolls over in his sleep, settling comfortably on his stomach. Vigy's bed is empty, the blankets unruffled. Her clothes are nowhere to be seen. But her heroes are, which is a good thing, since it means Vigy will be home eventually. Pericles says goodnight to them and climbs into bed, snuggling into the hollow his weight has carved in the hard old mattress. He lies back, staring at the darkness above him, watching the ceiling slowly descend.

Mind his head, Mam pleaded as they manhandled the old man's coffin into the hearse, and they all gaped at her.

Miss Hudson switched off the light with a smart snap and he saw her moving along the river bank.

Got one, shouted Grandad, and then he slipped and went under and the astonished fish gaped at this monstrous intrusion.

Pericles poked his way along the river and caught the teacher who wriggled prettily in his net but who seemed to like it well enough, and the sky came down on him.

Pericles watches the ceiling come slowly down on him. It descends like this every night which confuses yet does not frighten him, but every morning it is as though it had never moved. He has been meaning to ask Big Mike about this but keeps putting it off as though something told him it was special to himself, a knowledge not to be shared. He closes his eyes. The little fox curls up snugly in its den. The old owl bows his head and dozes watchfully. One by one with sharp snaps the stars extinguish themselves leaving everything in darkness, in silence, in fretful peace.

Summer

In the deepest part of the woods the overhanging trees shut out all that is dry and harsh. Pericles enters the woods so silently that even the sentry crow, guarding the flock on that side, does not notice him: the old and mottled leader-crow himself has to give the raucous two-toned caw of alarm. At his signal the flock rises and scatters, then gathers high in the air above the trees, riding the rising column of warm air, waiting for the intruder to withdraw. Only the unfortunate sentry crow who failed in his duty does not join the wheeling flock: each time it approaches the furious leader banks sharply and drives it off.

Oh my God, cries Miss Hudson.

Rapist, yelled Poppy Burn.

Oh no not that, cried Mam.

Pericles feels great sorrow for the outcast, morose and all alone, bewildered by the terrible fate which has overtaken him so suddenly.

Well, said Miss Hudson cheerfully, tomorrow we start our summer holiday, isn't that wonderful?

The children cheer loudly, holding the noise as long as their breath lasts.

And what are we all going to do for the next two and a half months? Miss Hudson would be grateful if they told her please.

The children hid their faces and giggled to themselves.

Pericles watched the teacher carefully.

I'll tell you what *I'm* going to do, shall I?

Yes, Miss, the children chorus.

Well, I'm going to spend the first eight weeks doing something I've been promising myself I would do for years . . .

– ?

I'm going to read all the books I've wanted to read but never found the time to.

Uhhh, groaned the children, who didn't think much of that.

And then, Miss Hudson added smiling, I'm going to Greece for ten glorious days.

Ohhhh, chanted the children, approving something that sounded much more promising.

Now, who can tell me where Greece is?

There, said Aoife Dowling, pointing dramatically out of the window.

Miss Hudson smiled kindly. Thank you Aoife. But could you be a little more specific?

Aoife didn't think she could, and Miss Hudson for some reason was not about to tell them, specifically or otherwise, the location of Greece, but she did say she was going to Hydra and Poros and possibly Crete but that depended on time.

The clock whirred and the thrush thumped its heart eleven times, panting.

Pericles walks on leaving the crows behind. A hen goon shoots out of the reeds on his left and breaks suddenly in mid-water: on one side of her a chick no bigger than a robin halts in unison. The boy hardly notices them. He is distracted by Miss Hudson's white belly in the water underneath the birds but for some reason it is now scarless, but still very smooth and white and round and nicely pretty.

Miss Hudson hit him in the face with all her strength and he stopped smiling.

And when we start school in September I'll be able to tell you all about my adventures, she said. And I expect all of you to tell me what *you've* been up to.

A little to the right on the opposite side of the river is the place where Pericles had enjoyed Poppy Burn: he smiles quietly in amused recognition.

I'm going straight to tell your Dad, Poppy yelled.

Sometime before that: Take me to the woods, Pericles, please.

Soon, said Pericles. I'm not ready.

Ready for what?

You'll see. Or someone would, thought Pericles, and pushed her into the reeds under him.

You keep well away from that Poppy Burn, Dad warned.

Pericles heard Dad roaring for him like a bull and saw Poppy Burn and her father walking away from the farmhouse.

Where's that bloody fool, Dad bellowed. Pericles!

Don't, Bill, Mam pleaded. Be careful. You know what he did —

Just let him try any of that shit on me and *I'll* kill *him*, Dad shouted.

Pericles smiled.

Pericles killed Grandad, the twins chorused.

What's he done now, Big Mike wanted to know so he would still know everything.

What's he done? Only gone and had it away with that Poppy Burn.

Pericles had it off with Poppy Burn? asked Big Mike incredulously. Christ, I never thought he had it in him.

Had it in Poppy Burn what's more, snorted Dad. Bloody did it and all. After me warning him a thousand times to keep away from her. Where the hell is he? Pericles — !

Dad caught him when he was in bed asleep and dragged him downstairs, out of the house and into the barn. For some obscure reason Dad always administered punishment in the barn as though he felt pain might defile the home. In the barn he whipped Pericles with an old riding crop, grunting with each stroke, great streams of sweat running down his jaw. The hens took flight from the rafters, showering them both with feathers and hard bullets of excrement. Pericles stood quite still under the lashes and smiled tightly at his father.

I'll bloody soon knock that smile off your face, Dad promised, his breath rasping as the whip cut into the boy's back and stung savagely.

It could have been worse, Mam tried. I mean she could have been pregnant.

I warned him, Dad insisted sullenly, furious that neither his words nor whippings appeared to have made any impression. How in the name of God do you get anything into his head?

She probably led him into it, Mam kept trying. You said yourself she was open to anyone.

But I warned him, the damn fool, Dad insisted, feeling that Mam was in some way about to get the better of the argument.

He doesn't always hear us, you know, Mam said.

Bloody hears us all right when he wants to.

Anyway, what's done is done, and it's too late now to do anything about it, Mam said.

Some consolation that is, remarked Dad, but he let the matter drop for the moment.

Had your nuts, then, Pericles, Big Mike observed later that night in bed.

Pericles said nothing.

Proper little fucker I bet you are. How the hell did you know where to put it?

I saw you, said Pericles.

Me?

And Vigy?

Jesus, you haven't told anyone, have you?

Pericles kept Big Mike waiting, enjoying, if not fully understanding the fact that he had somehow got Big Mike under his control. Finally, he shook his head. No, he said.

Big Mike heaved with relief. You're not a bad bugger really, he said almost tenderly. Enjoyed it, did you?

What?

You and Poppy of course.

That — I suppose so.

Don't you know?

I didn't think about it.

Proper little fucker you are I bet, said Big Mike again, and there was something that smacked of admiration in his voice.

Pericles chuckles happily to himself and thinks how odd it is that just the sound of his own quiet laughter can remind him of how he sat high in a tree and chuckled to himself as he watched Miss Hudson stride down the path that skirted the wood, wearing what he had once heard her describe as her 'sensible walking shoes'. Tricia loved this time of year, particularly when she had nothing to do but stroll alongside the great trees which seemed anchored to their shadows, their leaves filtering the sunlight and turning the woods a glorious shade of pollen. The mood was abruptly broken by a tallish man (who, she giddily decided, had been up to no good behind one of the trees only to be disturbed by her footsteps and jump smartly out on to the path) with straight dark hair going a rather distinguished grey at the temples but receding in the front, dressed despite the heat in a greatcoat which looked as though it might not have seen service since the dispersal of the Polish cavalry. The space between the discoloured crown of his loftily raised black homburg and the top of his head seemed to Tricia still to be fully occupied by something, the ghost perhaps of some perpetual remorse, or the memory of some almost forgotten happiness that he kept secreted under his hat but which now was forgetfully exposed and dazzled by the unaccustomed light. He was straddling the path in front of her, smiling generously, head tilted to one side as though he was having difficulty taking his bearings, his green slightly bloodshot eyes expressing an inquisitive emotion stranded between delight and dismay. He wavered, his stance exposing the broad blue-and-white stripes of his pyjama-tops, and black trousers with an elegant line of twisted braid down each seam. He gave the distinct impression that he had leaped from bed in response to some overwhelming urge and grabbed the first garments that came to hand. He came forward with eyes brightening, hand outstretched, his mouth clinging desperately to the evaporating semblance of an engaging smile, came forward with a lurching stride almost as though some invisible but determined hand, firmly planted in the small of his back, was pushing him against his will in her direction.

Good afternoon to you, young lady.

Good afternoon, Father.

A small constitutional?

Ah, yes. You could say that, Father. Isn't it glorious?

It is. It is indeed. You know I always feel that in sunshine there is another person who thinks for you, puts out your mental deckchairs, opens all the mind's windows, as it were, to let us enjoy a little spiritual sunbathing. Hmm?

I'm sorry, Father. I don't quite understand –

Nor I, more's the pity, Father Redmond sighed regretfully as the thought receded with something he might have described as Arnold's 'melancholy long withdrawing roar' had he been quite sober.

Actually, Father, I was thinking of coming to see you. I – Oh?

I wanted to talk to you about one of the children.

Suffer not, escaped Father Redmond before he could contain it and he remembered wrapping his coat tightly about him to resist the bitter wind and tramping the streets of his very first parish, side-stepping the wild steam blowing from the pavement grates over which ragged children, all homeless and unwanted except perhaps by the police, were preparing to bed themselves down and spend a fitful night under their cover of tattered cardboard and newspapers; yet none, even at that early stage of his ministry when zeal should still have pulsated in his veins, none as homeless as he, pursued down those nameless tear-filled streets by a sorrowing wind that called his name. But, somehow, it was always the next morning in the nick of time and he was having a therapeutic tipple and remembering to tell himself not to remember anything or –

– nicely, not that I haven't tried, Tricia Hudson was saying.

I'm sure you have, Father Redmond consoled her, which struck him as a sensible and non-commital enough reply. Almost immediately, however, he had second thoughts for an awkward silence fell between them for which he was undoubtedly responsible: a silence as infectious as a yawn and begetting a whispering stillness in the woods which in turn spawned a more general attentive silence. For once, incredibly, rescue was at hand however, in the shape of a small memory which dragged its feet across his mind. You wanted to speak to me about one of the children?

Yes, I just told you, Father. About Pericles Stort.

Ah, the immovable impenetrable Pericles Stort. Extraordinary boy! Do you know he is named after a brand of horse fodder? Amazing, isn't it? Well, almost. Pegasus, really, but either his parents couldn't remember that or things got mixed up along the way – and they do tend to, don't they – so they settled for Pericles. At least, that's what I'm led to believe.

You can't be serious!

Oh, but I am. And who knows, maybe it's all for the best – he's hardly a Tom or a Dick or a Harry, now is he?

I wouldn't have thought so, Tricia Hudson laughed gaily.

Quite. Or maybe, on the other hand, and this is quite possible – maybe his parents knew exactly what they were doing.

I doubt that, Tricia said ruefully. I think he has a pretty hard time of it at home. Particularly with his father.

Really? I exorcized him once, Father Redmond mentioned casually.

– ?

The boy, I mean, although –

You *what*?

I beg your pardon?

You *exorcized* him?

Who?

Pericles!

Exorcized? Me? Oh, no –

But you just said –

What did I just say?

That you did exorcize him.

Ah, what I meant was, I was *supposed* to exorcize him – but I couldn't, could I?

I should think not. What a horrible idea!

Such an unlikely place for Beelzebub to set up shop, Father Redmond kept talking – unless the demons are having a housing shortage, infernal mortgage problems would you think?

But what did happen, Father? What *did* you do?

And then again they are such vulnerable targets for wickedness, not only from devils, I might add. It always seems to be the innocent who get taken over, get seduced, get raped.

Raped?

– in a manner of speaking. He noticed he was starting to ramble and, thumping himself stoutly on the chest as though curing hiccups, pulled himself together. In any case, he continued, his eyes filling with boyish impudence, I decided I had to do *something* to put his parents' minds at ease so I performed a little ceremony of my own creation which I thought might fit the bill. I was pretty good too, even if I do say so myself. Goodness, you should have seen them jump when I roared with all my ecclesiastical solemnity, 'Begone Satan.' Father Redmond began to shake with uncontrollable laughter and even Tricia, who up to that point had been considerably shocked by the priest's revelations, found herself giggling.

I do believe, Father Redmond said finally, I do believe the boy alone knew what I was up to – and God, perhaps. What about him?

Oh, Pericles. I thought you meant – he came to see me.

And?

That's it. He came to see me. Or so he said. Nothing else. He just wanted to look at me.

Ah, said Father Redmond and nodded vaguely. He had a feeling things were going to get quite out of hand if he was not very careful.

And that's all he did, father. Just look at me until – well, he also wanted to touch me but there seemed to be nothing very wrong with that.

I don't think *he* would think it wrong –

I meant *I* didn't feel it was wrong.

Ah, said Father Redmond aware that this procession of monosyllables was all that was demanded of him for the moment and that they were being used by this delightful young lady as punctuation marks for her thoughts, as it had seemed to him not so very long ago (or, for that matter, a very long time ago) the occasional exclamation had been uttered most grate- fully by his friend the bishop as he struggled to respond to Father Redmond's: What would *you* recommend, my dear Lord Bishop, for a chronic, inevitable, often but not always enjoyable case of delirium tremens?

Ah, said the Bishop guardedly.

Surely in one of those sanctimonious tomes which you refer to so familiarly there is a paragraph, a sentence, a mere word which might give us a clue?

Hm, said the Bishop.

Or, like Darwin, are we committed to some long drawn-out voyage of discovery?

We? asked the Bishop good-humouredly.

Well, me, then. Am me committed?

You may have a point there, Denis, the Bishop smiled.

Ah. I see. Very devious of you, Matthew, but it wasn't quite the sort of committal I was referring to.

I know. Still –

– nor was it a Freudian slip.

I suppose not. Still – as I was about to say – it would be one answer to your problem. Temporary, of course.

Temporary answers never –

That's not what I mean, Denis.

I know, I know, Matthew, Father Redmond, said, giving this macabre conversation a jocular slant by grinning and giving the Bishop's sleeve a friendly tug.

I simply wanted to take the boy in my arms and hold him, a voice somehow familiar but too high-pitched to be episcopal was saying to him, and with great agility, he was proud to note, he coped brilliantly and summoned forth another exclamation from his private reservoir:

Ah, he said.

Hold him and love him –

Ah –

– and console him, Father.

Suddenly something more substantial was required: but why should that trouble you, Father Redmond asked.

Well, you see –

They strike me as eminently noble not to mention natural reactions –

You see, there was more to it than that, Father.

Alas, there always is, Father Redmond said not unkindly. It has always been man's torment that just when the most awful problems seem to be on the point of energetic solution –

It was as if I *had* actually held and loved him once. I simply cannot explain it any other way, Tricia Hudson confessed. A procession of thoughts, like small elderly dons, filed through her mind and in her mind, too, she was seated on a bench in a city park. She had always used the same bench set in the landscaped curve of a flowerbed planted with scarlet ger-aniums and purple fuchsias, smiling longingly at any small child who chanced to look her way, obscurely aware that her regular and strange behaviour made the other frequent visitors to the park eye her and chatter among themselves. I *think* – but it's ridiculous, isn't it? – she asked now, but I think, I really *do* think it has something to do with his eyes.

His eyes? Father Redmond sounded alarmed.

Yes. What he says with them, said Tricia.

What he says with them?

Yes, haven't you ever noticed them, father?

Father Redmond had, and he admitted as much if somewhat reluctantly. He admitted also, but only to himself, that while he could be considered an expert on optical illusions he was imperceptibly being dragged into spheres he had no desire to penetrate at this moment. It was with great courage therefore that he pursued the topic, however briefly. I never did believe that the eyes are the mirror of the soul, he stated with impressive clerical authority. But I grant you there *is* something in that boy's eyes, something, I think, which allows us to look at ourselves as we used to be . . . Lord, it *is* getting hot, he added removing an almost invisible insect from his sleeve, holding it aloft and staring at it. Cuttysark's niggit, would you think? he asked.

I'm sorry – ?

Which reminds me – perhaps if you walked with me to the rectory I could offer you some, eh, lemonade? And you could tell me more of what is worrying you?

Pericles stares into the dull brown water of the river and wonders, but with not great interest, what more they had had to say of him.

Tricia Hudson tried to settle herself comfortably into the over-stuffed Victorian sewing chair, keeping a wary eye on the priest who now appeared wholly occupied in some elaborate game of hity-tity with a collection of bottles in a heavy oak corner cupboard.

The truth is, father, she ventured, raising her voice as much to drown the clinking as to attract his attention, the truth is I sometimes – I *know* it's absurd but I just can't help it – I sometimes believe he's *part* of me.

It is not important *what* we believe only *that* we believe, quoted the priest from the bowels of the cupboard. Goebbels said that, you know. Amazing, isn't it? But it doesn't really apply here, I suppose, he added uselessly. What did apply, however, was that he pulled off the outrageous covenage he was currently involved in: transferring quantities of what he hoped was Vat 69 (flippantly referred to as the Pope's telephone number during his seminary days), into an empty Lucozade bottle. Unfortunately, he had made so many substitutions on so many occasions that he was now totally confused. A glass of sherry? he suggested.

That would be nice, said Tricia.

Father Redmond handed her a glass of sherry having first, with studied ostentation, placed a Lucozade bottle and tumbler on the floor beside his chair (a monstrous buttoned leather throne, shabby and worn, great chunks of horsehair oozing from its sores, giving that tousled impression of an unmade bed) and sat down opposite her a gleam of gratified optimism flickering in his eyes. Your very good health, he toasted her, drinking deeply.

And yours, Father. Father, I need your *help* –

The mood of optimism and happy relief took flight and vanished completely. Father Redmond realized that what he had hoped all along, preposterous though he knew it to be, was that this young teacher would come to *his* rescue even if only to lead him by the hand through the gathering hordes of whiffmagigs which jostled him relentlessly, through the grey-haired durgans which feasted and grew obese on the weariness of his mind, through the simmering crowd of poltroons whose every face was his own, and away from the assembled sinister Greeks (for some inexplicable reason) trying so desperately to sell him flagons of rompney and sometimes (but not often enough) succeeding, away and along the dusty lonely road which for all the world resembled the grey broad back that God had turned upon him. Instantly, consciously, Father Redmond dismissed God. It ran through his head that he could perhaps create some diversion at this moment from the hopelessness he felt was all that he was capable of offering this young woman, yet he did nothing about it. Instead, he drained his tumbler in one swift gulp and poured himself another. This done he presented to the room a face wreathed in a wide disarming smile filled, he was sure, with the promise of deep concern and compassion. How can *I* help you, child? he asked.

I'm so frightened, Father, Tricia confessed quietly. *Really* frightened.

Ah –

Can you understand, father?

Understand? Alas, poor fright, I know him well! Of the boy?

Good heavens no. Tricia Hudson gave a tiny nervous laugh. Then, gradually, her face tightened. Of myself mostly, I suppose, she added almost whispering.

Father Redmond tapped his celluloid collar with his index finger trying desperately to think of something purposeful to say. He took another mouthful of whiskey and let the liquid trickle slowly down his throat but even that didn't seem to help. He could locate nothing in his mind which made any sense at this awful moment. Fortunately, as it turned out, nothing was expected of him.

– as I've already told you, the teacher was saying, there are times when I ache to hold him in my arms but – well, then I want more than just that. I want him – I *need* him to love me –

But my poor dear child we all need to be loved, Father Redmond heard his voice say. My good Lord, we all need to be loved every bit as much as we need to love.

You don't understand, father –

I'm certainly trying.

I know you are. I'm sorry. The silly thing is that I feel that if he did love me it would be just as though I loved myself. Do I make any sense at all, father?

I'm afraid you do.

Is there something wrong with me that I long so much to be

loved and above all to love myself?

God commands us to love –

Ourselves?

– others as ourselves which is the same thing I think, is it not? The other side of the coin being that the commandments such as we are instructed to follow seem more often than not to be implemented by idiots. But that, as they say, is another story.

Father, please help me – please?

Father Redmond looked quickly away from Tricia Hudson's pleading face. Far back in his mind a nicotined voice cajoled '*Thelis Nadia?*' At first he saw only the sultry Thessalonikan features of the girl in the tight red dress who confronted him. Some reckless suicidal power was urging him on, driving him through the open door and into the darkened room, one room of a dozen that gave off the landing, yet all the while he remained passionately aware of the inevitable consequences he would never be able to undo. So this was it, he thought, the final rejection. He could prevent it even now but he was too jaded, too drunk to do anything about it. Perhaps some God with whom he had once been on quite familiar terms would offer some advice. He peered about the tiny room, listening: no god had any opinion on the matter, it seemed. The room itself, in which the only light was a small electrified crucifix with the jitters before a half life-sized statue of some obscure Orthodox saint visibly suffering from the arrows piercing his breast, was sparsely furnished. It could have been his room in the seminary all those years ago had it not been for that incongruous be-arrowed image and the enormous poster covering one third of the wall over the bed on which the words, barely discernible in the crucified light, appeared: WHERE THERE IS GREAT POWER OR GREAT GOVERNMENT, OR GREAT LOVE AND COMPASSION, THERE IS ERROR FOR WE PROGRESS BY FAULT. The bed beneath this oddly disturbing legend was unmade and mildly rancid though it, too, resembled the tubular metal-framed cots favoured in seminaries. He noticed on the table by it an almost full bottle of brandy, and the fact that he progressed by default conveniently cancelled any misgivings: he made for the bottle and drank until he had finished it. The girl had been undressing methodically, chattering to him in Greek which, for no obvious reason, she seemed certain he understood, and now moved towards him, clasping her arms about his neck and drawing him down on the bed. Her legs, her breasts, her soft plump hands with their violet varnished nails, her entire body, her sad, economically passionate heart – all these were the materialization of his every adolescent dream, but even as his whole being twitched and shivered with excitement the pleasure was draining from him and slipping away into a desolate, bleak and abandoned darkness without a glimmer of light in it. The heaving, perspiring body beneath him with its tang of garlic and cheap perfume was a mere abstraction, a daemonic apparatus for blasphemous, sickening, illicit orgasm. It was total renunciation. It was physical pain. It was the mental terror of waking in the dawnless hours with the awful knowledge that he was expected to perform the greatest miracle while his brain tried bravely to concentrate and contemplate transubstantiation but his throat cried out only for the first sweet easing taste of altar wine. It was the struggle to keep his hands from shaking (and failing dismally); it was his faltering steps down to the communion rail where hungry recipients shot their eager tongues at him like monstrous gargoyles. It was all this and a lot more, he knew, as he penetrated the woman who groaned beneath him: the only thing left to him now this searing ragged organ. Oh, God, wherein the difference between the groans of love and the groans of certain death? Oh, sweet and generous Jesus, help me!

How can *I* help you? Father Redmond asked Tricia Hudson, nodding his head in response to some request he seemed vaguely to recall.

I don't think you can, Father.

Ah, said Father Redmond; hurt, but more relieved than he

was hurt. He stared at the teacher, waiting for her to speak again. For the moment she was distracted, her eyes fixed on a strange arrangement of ragwort and zinnias in a pewter mug on the mantelpiece, her brow furrowed.

In fact I *know* you can't, father, she said sadly.

I'm sorry, child.

I think I really knew there was nothing you could do before I even spoke to you.

Am I that transparent? Father Redmond thought he heard himself ask.

But I had to ask, didn't I? Tricia concluded.

Father Redmond nodded again and made as if to speak, opening and closing his mouth in a peculiar masticating gesture. His eyes were swimming in tears and there was nothing he could do about it, nothing he could reasonably think of at any rate. And as though to distract attention from this predicament he took to plucking wads of horsehair from the arm of his chair, letting each handful float to the floor by opening his fingers wide, waiting patiently for each wad to land before continuing the disembowelment. And he was beginning to shake again: those great heaving shudders he had noticed so often at gravesides when distant relatives and fairweather friends, suddenly face to face with the grim inexplicable finality of death, strove to contain their theatrically induced sorrow within themselves lest they be thought to exceed their role and usurp the inalienable right to passionate grief of the principal mourners. Through his tears, surmounting the almost insurmountable obstacle of his shaking body, Father Redmond suddenly held a whisp of horsehair aloft and surveyed it studiously: the rudder of Tamoshanter's horse, would you think? he asked. Then he leaned forward, his elbows on his knees, and buried his face in his hands.

Instinctively, Tricia Hudson began to reach out towards the sobbing priest, but her reaction was cut short. Slowly, unbelievably it was her father leaning forward in the chair opposite her, his head buried in his hands, weeping pitifully. I wanted so much to save him, he was saying through his fingers, the words drowning to a whisper in his plight. Don't you see it would have made everything worth while?

Pericles stops wondering about the priest and Miss Hudson and about what else they might have said of him. He reaches under his pullover and over his shoulder and fingers the welts left by Dad's whipping. They feel rough and scabby like lengths of baling twine soldered to his skin, but in no way trouble him.

It could have been worse, Mam said for the umpteenth time.

I warned the stupid bugger, said Dad likewise.

She's only a slut anyway, said Big Mike who knew everything.

But I warned him, said Dad despairingly.

Better he practised on her, said Big Mike, than to have tried and have it off with one of the others in the village. Christ, *everyone's* had a go at *her* –

That's enough, Big Mike, said Dad, suddenly nervous.

I was only saying –

We know what you were saying and I said it's enough.

Pericles feels unusually sad: he is upset by the thought of the unfortunate crow which tonight must roost alone. He jumps to his feet: he feels late, but for what he cannot quite remember. Or is he ahead of time. The clock clops once and stops. He retraces his steps along the river bank, running towards something or away from something. He cannot be sure. Maybe that is why he is late or early.

He ran all the way and found himself at school. He was late. But at the same time right on time. On time, at any rate, to hear Miss Hudson ring her handbell vigorously.

The bell has gone, said Miss Hudson sharply.

Yes, ma'am.

Whatever happened to you today?

I'm not sure, ma'am.

Not sure? – Never mind.

114

Thank you, ma'am.

You'd better go home again now.

Yes, ma'am.

Goodbye, then, until after the holidays.

Goodbye, ma'am.

And see to it that you don't play truant next term.

I will, ma'am.

Or I'll have to speak to your parents, said Miss Hudson turning away from him with unaccustomed abruptness.

Yes, ma'am, said Pericles, hurt.

Have a nice holiday anyway. I'll see you in September.

Before that, ma'am.

Why before that, Pericles?

I'm sure, ma'am.

Sure? Sure of what?

Sure I'll see you before September, ma'am. I'd like to.

Well, that's nice to hear. But I'll be away so I don't think our paths will cross –

Paths, ma'am?

A manner of speaking –

Oh, I thought you meant something else, ma'am.

No.

I see, ma'am.

They eyed each other briefly.

Well, goodbye again, Pericles.

Goodbye, ma'am.

Drat the boy! Miss Tricia Hudson made the entry carefully in her diary, a great thick leather-bound affair with what looked like a family crest intaglioed on the cover, and a small padlock in brass. The first two months of the summer had slipped away in much the manner she had expected apart from one disquieting entanglement with the priest; but even that, once she thought about it rationally, seemed to fit naturally into the order of things. She read the books she promised herself she would read, devouring a little Proust and Balzac, hacking her way through the mystifying verbiage of Joyce and Beckett, laughing merrily along with Salinger – what a fabulous name Zooey was! – and she was about to assist with the harpooning of Moby Dick. She had deliberately postponed reading Melville until last since even the title sent skittish laughter racing through her brain. All this was far from Tricia's mind, however, as she painstakingly filled several pages of her diary, carefully choosing her words as though they were to be read by someone other than herself. She reread her entry and smiled wistfully at her pretentions although feeling at the same time a strange release, a sense of attainment. It was as though, out of her few fatuous remarks, she had derived strength. Her mind was clear. She felt free to enjoy her forthcoming trip to Greece in peace.

Pericles races through the woods, ducking and dodging the lower branches, leaping over gullies and rotting trunks. The newly invested sentries summon the alarm and the band of crows rises up over the trees and circles until the boy has passed and the all clear sounded. Pericles runs as fast as he can, his heart thumping.

Thump.

Not again, Bill, not now.

She likes it well enough.

Wow.

Carefully, Tricia Hudson packs her suitcase. There is an odd finality in the way she places each article of clothing inside, the exaggerated precision of Hollywood actresses of the late forties, alone in their sumptuous attics, as they stow away in metal trunks the memorabilia and trinkets of their celluloid husbands so unkindly removed by the fiendish orientals. Tricia Hudson starts: for goodness sake I'm going on *holiday* not to my execution, she tells herself, and throws the few remaining garments unceremoniously into the case, slamming down the lid. There are still several hours to pass between now and the time the ferry leaves for the mainland. She sits on the edge of her bed beating out the rhythm of a drum on the simulated leather suitcase. And the sight of Father Redmond, head in hands, looms into her mind. I'm so *sorry*, he had said later.

Oh, no. It's all my fault. I shouldn't have – I didn't realize –

No, of course not, he had reassured her and smiled, perhaps feeling safe on the mutual ground of half-admitted failure. How could you?

Anyway, I'm sure I'll feel better when I get away for a little.

Get away?

Yes. I'm going to Greece for ten days.

Ah –

Perhaps a break would do you good, Father?

I think not, Father Redmond shook his head slowly. I've tried that too. I always seem to bring myself along with me. Part of my excess baggage for which I have to pay the inevitable toll. Overburdened, he added mostly to himself. And somehow that seems quite intolerable when I am removed from the things I know. Like being blind, I suppose, and having everything strategically placed in one's own home and suddenly finding some goblin has broken in and shifted everything around.

Away shoots the goon and her chick as Pericles races on. He stops briefly when he comes to the cornfield, now shorn and ugly. He eyes the stubble and wonders again why Dad cut the golden sheaves which were so beautiful

beautiful Pericles

and left the field bare with no places for small animals to hide from the marauding owls. He runs on, out over the stubble, vaulting the wall that surrounds the field, and down the lane. He knows where he is going now.

Got to learn the way himself, Dad insisted. I'm not driving that moron to school every day of the week.

Just this once, said Mam; and just this once, said Eileen Ferris to Patrick Bullock, just this once let us say goodbye without promises or lies.

Poppy Burn ran towards him, her mouth open: Take me to the woods, she pleaded.

Pericles rests, panting, trying to catch his breath, when he reaches the gate leading into the school yard. After several minutes and breathing normally he opens the gate and walks in, closes it behind him and puts the latch down properly. He smooths down his hair, wiping any greasiness from the palms of his hands by rubbing them roughly on the seat of his trousers, and crosses the yard deliberately. Firmly he knocks on the door of the house adjoining the school, the house from which the sun shines at night without creating daylight, and waits.

'Why, Pericles! I was just –' Miss Hudson begins, glancing over her shoulder in the direction of the suitcase. 'What is it you want?'

'I've got something for you, ma'am.'

'For me? Oh.' The teacher's voice rises slightly. She seems pleased.

'Yes, ma'am.'

'How kind of you. Whatever is it?'

'I couldn't bring it with me, ma'am.'

'Well then I don't see –'

'You have to come and see it. But I know you'll like it, ma'am.'

'I'm sure I shall, Pericles, but I can't get away right now. I'm –'

'I know you'll like it, ma'am.'

'Well, tell me where it is –'

'Not too far away.'

'Don't you sass your teacher, Dad warned.

She's a proper lady and you call her ma'am, his mother said.

' – ma'am,' Pericles adds quickly.

'You mean you want me to come with you? This minute? I'm sorry, Pericles, I really don't think I can –'

'It won't take long, ma'am. Honestly. No time at all. And I

118

know you'll like it a lot.'

Take me to the woods, begged Poppy.

I'm not ready, said Pericles. When I'm ready I'll take you.

'I simply don't have the time, Pericles. I hate to disappoint you but I do have the ferry to catch.'

'It won't take long,' the boy assures her.

Pericles watched Big Mike and Vigy on the bed and tucked away their contortions in his mind in case they should ever prove to be useful.

'Not long at all, ma'am,' he reassures her.

'You don't seem to understand, Pericles. I have to catch the ferry or I'll miss the connecting train and then the plane and if that happens my whole holiday will be messed up.'

'I won't let you miss anything, ma'am.'

'I'm *sorry*, Pericles. I simply cannot –'

' – please, ma'am.'

'Well –'

'Thank you, ma'am.'

'I haven't said I'd come –'

'But you will, ma'am, won't you – please?'

'Oh, all right, Pericles. I suppose it's the least I can do. You were very kind to think of me.'

'Think of you, ma'am?'

'Why yes – your present –'

'Oh.'

'Or was I mistaken – ?'

'Oh, no, ma'am. No you weren't. You'll like it.'

'I'll just throw on a cardigan and then I'll be right with you.'

'That's fine, ma'am. Thank you.'

'Just wait here a tick. I won't be a moment.'

'Yes, ma'am.'

He wedged Grandad carefully under the pole and nobody found poor him for three days.

'Here I am,' announces Miss Hudson cheerfully. 'I'm all ready. Lead on McDuff, I'm in your hands.'

'That's right, ma'am,' agrees Pericles smiling. 'You just follow me. It's not too far at all.'

'Just as long as you don't let me miss my ferry. We'll be back within, say, an hour, won't we?'

Pericles says nothing.

'Won't we, Pericles?' Miss Hudson insists.

'If you want to, ma'am.'

'I certainly do.'

'Yes, ma'am. All right.

He leads the way with Miss Hudson, feeling very young and gay, thinking of humming to herself, tagging along close behind. It is a glorious afternoon filled with summer warmth and refreshed by a good drenching of overnight rain.

'Tell me, Pericles, what have you planned for the rest of your summer holidays?' the teacher suddenly wants to know.

'I don't know yet, ma'am. Walk maybe.'

'Just walk?' Miss Hudson chuckles in surprise. 'You can't really spend the next couple of weeks just walking, can you?'

'Oh, and sit, ma'am,' says Pericles logically.

'Good heavens. Just walk and sit? But that's something you do every day. Isn't there something special you want to do in holiday time?'

Pericles thinks. 'No, ma'am,' he confesses eventually.

'Well, let me put it this way. Forget about holidays. Isn't there something exciting or adventurous or just plain silly that you've always longed to do but never got round to?'

Pericles stops, turns, and stares at the teacher: ' – ?'

'There must be *something* which interests you in a very special way. Everybody has their own little secret desires, you know.'

Pericles turns on his heel and starts walking again, his head down, thinking hard about the teacher's question. The muffled clock thuds and Grandad screams that he can't swim and Pericles watches him in his mind's eye as he drowns again. You know what you are? Poppy Burn demands. You're a bloody rapist, she yelled and Dad dragged him off to the barn and chained him up by the neck and the chickens flew in his face with unsheathed talons forcing him to close his eyes tightly and when he looked again he lay in bed with the chickens scattered about him in all directions their lovely white feathers flecked with red blood like the mare's chest was flecked with eggfroth in the summer when she came in from ploughing.

' – something *so* special you tell nobody about it and would do it every single day if you could and never get tired of doing it –' Miss Hudson is saying.

'Every day?' Pericles asks over his shoulder.

'Yes. Well, no. You're quite right. *Anything* would get boring if you did it *every* day.'

'Yes, ma'am.'

'Let's say almost every day, then,' says Miss Hudson, mildly surprised that what had started as a perfectly ordinary chatty question had somehow developed into something so confusing.

'Like what, ma'am?'

'Like anything. Oh, I don't know. I think we had better drop the subject.'

'Why, ma'am?' Pericles asks, still thinking very hard.

'I just don't think it was a very good idea of mine.'

'Yes it was, ma'am.'

'I'm glad *you* think so, Pericles,' says Miss Hudson, her heavy sarcasm wasted on the boy.

'I'm still thinking, ma'am.'

'Oh?'

'There is one thing, ma'am.'

'There is?'

'I'd like to give you something almost every day.'

'Something?'

'Yes, ma'am. Like I'm going to give you now.'

'Oh, a present. I see. To me? Why to me?'

'Because.'

'You're much too good to me, Pericles. You mustn't spoil me, you know.'

Don't sass the teacher.

She's a proper lady. You call her ma'am.

And she smelled of babysoap on weekdays.

Feel this.

'Goodness it *is* warm!' exclaims Miss Hudson. She takes off her cardigan. 'Do we have much further to go?'

'Oh, no, ma'am,' the boy assures her, sensing the disquiet in her voice. 'Just across the field and then a little bit into the woods. But it's nice and cool in there, ma'am.' He turns his head and smiles encouragement.

'Into the woods? Oh, dear. I don't think –'

'Just a little way in,' Pericles insists.

'Well – well, all right – if it is just a little way –'

'Oh it is, ma'am.'

You know what happens if you put that thing in me, asked Poppy.

Pericles sees the new sentries before they spot him and he points them out to the teacher. 'They warn the other crows that we're coming,' he explains. 'They bark like dogs when they see us. They usen't to worry about me but they do now,' he adds, puzzled.

'Maybe it's me they don't like.'

'No. That's not it. They just changed their minds about me.'

'Whyever should they do that, Pericles?'

'Knowing,' says Pericles mysteriously.

'Goodness!' But there seems little good in what is happening to her now. Suddenly, the happiness of her mood is fading. The cooling summer breeze has lost its way in the huge primeval trees and only sighs occasionally. The woods have become unusually oppressive and humid. And how silent. Not a sound. Not a hint of birdsong, or any other song for that matter, reaches her ears. Nothing but the muffled suction of their own feet as they penetrate deeper into the brooding quiet, that eerie watchful quiet that Albrecht must have sensed while waiting for Giselle. How terribly wrong it has all become.

'Are you coming, Ma'am?' Pericles asks.

'Oh – oh, yes, Pericles. I'm sorry. I was miles away. Of course I'm coming.'

'It took me a long time to get this ready, Ma'am,' says Pericles shyly.

'It did? I wonder what it can be!'

'You'll see, Ma'am.'

'Goodness, you have me terribly excited!' Probably a bird's nest, she thinks, or some wild flowers, a small animal, a lamb, perhaps. But there seems nothing so gentle around her now. No lamb of God who takest away the sins of the world, she thinks wildly, inwardly flinching at her mockery. Yet that was precisely the trouble: everything from dumb animals to figments of Papal imaginations (conveniently called indulgences and issued as commercially as any trading stamp) eradicated the sin. But the bull, Pontific or merely crude, failed to remove the one torment that haunted her: the decimating, devouring guilt, the darkness that seeped into her very bones, the terror that could still awaken her in the night from that recurrent nightmare of abandoned children reaching out to her, beseeching; that terror which as a child she had been expected to display before the supposed wrath of God if only to satisfy her mother's fantasies. Often, lying trembling in a cold sweat, waiting for the insinuations of her nightmare to drift back into focus, she felt a great compassion for the ridiculous Catholic lamb since the poor stupid creature seemed so like herself, lured by that ironic Judas goat, by Judas people in her case with whom she only wanted to be friendly, who enticed her by encouraging that wish and by whom, because they desired only to humiliate her, she was finally ensnared.

'I'm so hot, Pericles. Are we nearly there?'

'Yes, ma'am. Honestly.'

You're too hot, said Big Mike who knew everything and

123

proceeded to seduce Vigy while Pericles watched and noted each contortion they made.

The twins snored softly, their arms about each other.

Pericles is watching, warned Vigy.

Don't matter, said Big Mike. He won't know what we're doing.

But Pericles tried it himself anyway: Wow, said Vigy; Wow, said Poppy; take me to the woods said someone.

The demoted drowsy crow eyes them sullenly from its perch, petulantly refusing to divulge their presence, and Pericles explains the drama of his explusion to the teacher.

'Well I never!' exclaims Miss Hudson. 'However did you learn all that about the birds?'

Pericles has no idea how he learned all that about the birds so he ignores the teacher's question. He just knows. Like animals know, he supposes.

Like some bloody animal he is, Dad complained bitterly. The way he creeps about and hides himself – it's not natural.

He's just a child playing his little games, Mam tried to reason. At least it keeps him out of trouble, doesn't it?

Dad snorted.

Play with it a little, Big Mike ordered Vigy for the third time.

Wow, said Vigy. You're much better than Big Mike. Much, much better – I can tell you that for sure, she added emphatically as Pericles cleaned off her huge breasts with his tongue and she cleaned off Pericles and the hay rustled with the shifting of curious small animals watching.

Pericles is watching, Vigy warned.

Don't matter, Big Mike insisted.

Watch how you dress him, Mam wailed. If you open those cuts again his best suit will be ruined.

But he's going to be buried in it anyway, isn't he? Nobody's ever going to see the suit again, silly, Vigy pointed out. That's not the point, Mam said defensively. And don't you dare call me silly.

124

For heaven's sake, Mam – Vigy began.

He's got to be neat and respectable for any emergency, Mam insisted.

I can't understand why we dress him at all. Waste of good clothes, really. He's not going to *need* them, you know, Mam.

Vigy! Mam gasped shocked. We can't bury him in nothing!

Why not? It's the way he was born. Anyway, where he's going clothes won't make a damn bit of difference.

Don't talk like that, Vigy, Mam said, crying again. No matter where he goes I'm not letting him go there naked, she added, as though nudity after death was a sure way to encourage celestial wrath.

Oh, for heaven's sake, Mam, Vigy exclaimed again – you're going soft in the head in your old age.

That's quite enough of your lip, girl, Mam snapped, suddenly annoyed, possibly with her own stupidity. It simply had not occurred to her that the good, practically unworn suit would never be seen again. Why ever did the boy do it, she asked of nobody in particular although she seemed to direct her question to the corpse which looked as good as new now that she had patched it up. That's something I'll never, never understand.

Could have been one of us the mad bugger chopped up, Dad informed anyone who felt like listening.

Big Mike felt like listening: Oh, thanks, he said – that'll sure make me sleep well!

I wouldn't sleep at all if I were you, Big Mike, Dad advised almost smiling and obviously gratified by his son's discomfort. You're sure to be next on the list, he added.

Shit, said Big Mike. You're the one who always whips him. Just let him try anything on me, warned Dad but his eyes were red and frightened.

Eileen's eyes were red and soulful as she opened the door of the farmhouse and saw Patrick Bullock standing there. Is it really you, Patrick, she asked.

Yes, Eileen.

You haven't changed, Eileen lied.

Nor have you, he lied back.

I've been promoted and sent here, Sergeant Bullock told her. And this was true although it was hardly the glad tidings he made it sound. All through the years he had been a good policeman; good and honest and trustworthy but totally uninspired which hardly mattered as long as serious crime in the metropolis meant the occasional car theft, rape, or child abuse. But when appalling violence crept in, when armed robbery, grim acts of terrorism and gruesome murders became almost commonplace, Constable Bullock found himself unable to cope, unable to cope both with a new conception of human brutality and with the new sophisticated gadgetry used to combat it. After a couple of pathetic blunders his superiors had decided it was time to do something about him. But what to do? *De*motion was out of the question since on the whole his record was excellent. A desk job was equally unthinkable since there was little doubt the ramifications of paper-work would be beyond him. And then, much to the relief of the Chief Inspector, someone had the inspired idea of posting him back to his native island. That would solve everything quite neatly since Constable Bullock would thus be out of harm's way and the post automatically carried the rank of Sergeant. Slow he may have been but Patrick Bullock knew there was little glory in his transfer. He accepted it graciously nevertheless, accepted it even willingly for he was a tired and disillusioned man, a failure by any standards; he recognized this posting as a last chance to preserve his dignity.

I came back, you see, he told Eileen.

But like I said, not in time, Patrick, Eileen told him wistfully.

No. Not in time. It's hard to believe you're so long married and with a houseful of children I hear.

Oh, yes. A houseful.

Are you happy, Eileen?

Bill Stort's been a good husband. I've never wanted for anything. I get by.

Are you happy? he asked again.

Happy? That's only a word, Patrick. How can we know if we're happy unless we've been sad? And I can't say I've had a lot of sadness in my life.

I'm glad. I often think of –

Shhh, Patrick, Eileen whispered, reaching her fingers towards his lips. Shhh, those days are secrets, precious secrets. If we speak of them they will shatter.

Perhaps you're right.

I'm right.

If you need me –

I know, Patrick. I'll call you.

I'll look in from time to time if I may –

'Oh, look, Pericles!' says Miss Hudson as a hen goon shoots from the reeds and dips to a halt in mid-stream, a chick by her side.

After her father's death Tricia had made a genuine, determined but useless effort to penetrate her mother's aloofness. Quite apart from her eccentric and hilarious incubations (Mother, do you *have* to take those eggs with you in your bra when you go *shopping*? Of course, Tricia. But you look so ridiculous! You can hardly expect me to abandon the little orphans, dear. But they're *eggs*, dammit. They're God's creatures, Tricia, and we don't all have the same chances in life that you've had) she had taken to shielding herself from criticism behind a protective wall of pessimism. Everything that happened was fate, or the hand of the Lord, and it was fruitless to try any alteration of that. She regarded Tricia with an ever more reproachful eye as though she had become one of fate's more cruel tribulations and gradually the atmosphere between the two women became covertly hostile. After her child was born Tricia moved, and direct contact with her mother almost ceased. From time to time in the years that followed Tricia's conscience pricked her and she wrote long chatty letters to her mother, filling page after page with trivia, pretending there had been no rift. She never got a reply, but this somehow made it easier to pretend that her mother really loved her and for her to write again.

'Yes, ma'am, goons,' explains Pericles.

'Goons? Gracious. I didn't know we had any goons around here.'

'Oh, yes, ma'am. Plenty,' says Pericles.

'Well you certainly do know a lot about the woods, don't you? I must get you to lead one of our nature-study classes next term. You would do that for me, wouldn't you?'

'If you want me to, ma'am,' the boy says and smiles, and picked his mother's shoulder free of loose grey hairs. 'We're nearly there now, ma'am,' he tells the teacher.

Tricia Hudson shades her eyes with one hand and stares ahead. The sun filters in auburn shafts between the trees yet it seems to get increasingly darker further on, but this could have been her jittery imagination: it could be her imagination, also, that makes her feel that every living creature in the woods is holding its breath and watching. Miss Hudson shivers. 'You were right, Pericles. It certainly is very much cooler in here,' she says. 'Yes, ma'am,' Pericles agrees. 'I told you it would be.' He knows the willow tree is not far away now and hopes that everything is in order. It should all be ready, he knows, but perhaps he has been expected to do something more. Abruptly he stops in his tracks.

'Why have we stopped?' the teacher wants to know: a small creature jibbers in the undergrowth and makes her jump.

Pericles tortures his boots into screaming.

Pericles, be quiet, said the teacher, annoyed.

Yes, ma'am. Sorry, ma'am.

I should think so too.

Yes, ma'am, said Pericles amiably.

'Pericles, why have we stopped?' Miss Hudson demands again.

Pericles bumped Grandad's arm and the knife hummed harmlessly into the tree-trunk as the squirrel laughed high above them. Damn you, boy, Grandad swore.

'I was just listening, ma'am,' Pericles explains.

'Oh, you heard that funny jibbery sound too. What was –'

'No, ma'am. Just listening.'

'To what, then?'

'Anything.' He leaps over the stream in a single graceful movement with no apparent effort, turns and watches the teacher.

Miss Hudson raises her eyebrows in conscious good-humoured mockery:

'I see. You want *me* to do that? Across the river and into the trees,' she says tightly.

'Yes, ma'am.'

Tricia Hudson jumps the stream awkwardly. She stumbles on landing and careers into the boy, almost bringing him down. 'Oops,' she cries nervously. 'I'm sorry. I'm certainly not as agile as you, am I? My age must be showing.'

Pericles smells the babysoap and says nothing.

'Oh, dear. I seem to have hurt my ankle,' the teacher says, trying her foot tentatively. 'It will be all right in a moment. I think I had better sit for a while, though.'

Pericles looks momentarily worried. 'Yes, ma'am. All right,' he says reluctantly.

'The rest will do us both good, anyway,' Tricia Hudson tells him. 'I am really quite tired.'

'Yes, ma'am.'

Tricia spreads her cardigan on the ground and lowers herself gingerly while Pericles hunkers down a little way off and stares into the distance. For the first time Tricia notices the incredible beauty of the boy's face: no smooth effeminate softness nor yet a handsomeness. It is more that indefinable peaceful innocence which should have abandoned him years ago; two lines of a poem lilt gently in her brain:

> *You have weaned me too soon*
> *You must nurse me again.*

'What are you thinking about, Pericles?'

'I don't know, ma'am,' Pericles says and seems to mean it.

'You look so lonely over there. Why don't you come and sit beside me on my cardigan?'

'Would you like that, ma'am?'

'Why, yes. Yes, Pericles, I would.'

'All right, ma'am.'

Pericles moves over to the teacher and sits beside her. He does not look at her but studies the leaves between his legs.

'I'll tell you what *I'm* thinking,' Miss Hudson volunteers generously. 'I'm thinking what a very nice, kind young man you are.'

Pericles turns his head, smiling. 'Nobody ever told me that, ma'am.'

'Well they jolly well should have. And I'm telling you now. Just look how kind you've been to me! Why you –'

'You're different, ma'am.'

'Different? Whatever do you mean?'

'I've known you so long, ma'am.'

'Only a year, Pericles. That's not so – '

'No, ma'am. Much longer than that. I've known you always.'

'Always?'

'Yes, ma'am. Always that I can remember, anyway.'

'But I only came here ten months ago, Pericles.'

'That doesn't matter, ma'am. Does it?'

'I think it does.'

'Not to me.'

'Now, Pericles, you mustn't be silly. You *can't* have known

130

me always. Why, you hadn't even *seen* me until – '

'Oh, I've seen you all the time, ma'am,' Pericles tells her and watched the ceiling come down on him.

'But this is ridiculous! I've certainly never seen you before I came here – '

'Haven't you, ma'am? I was sure you'd remember.'

'Remember what, Pericles, for heaven's sake?'

'Before.'

'Before *what*?' Tricia Hudson asks, her voice taking on a shrill note of panic.

Before you waved your hand and abandoned me, the boy seems to be saying. Before, too, you had the chance to call me Sefer and love me and be loved by me, before your love dried up and left you forever, forever searching . . . why did you send me away, Tricia, the voice persists. Could you not see that I was all you would ever have?

Tricia Hudson scrambles to her feet, trembling. 'I'm sorry, Pericles. I can't go on any more. I simply must get back. I'm late as it is.'

'That's all right, ma'am. We're here.'

'Here? Where?'

'We go in there.' Pericles points to the drooping willow branches and makes off towards them.

The teacher stands her ground, wetting her lips quickly with her tongue. 'In where?' she demands, her voice huskily frightened. 'I can't see anything to go in to.'

Pericles draws back the foliage like a conjuror displaying an empty cage at the start of some amazing illusion, and beckons her forward. 'It's inside, ma'am,' he explains patiently.

'Inside?' Tricia Hudson moves cautiously forward holding her cardigan tightly about her shoulders, both arms crossed over her breasts in what she had once wittily referred to as her Maidenform pose. 'What is inside, Pericles?'

The boy continues to hold back the branches for her with the quiet dignity of an aged footman, smiling. She peers tentatively through the opening. Inside it is cold, damp, and musty like an animal's den. Innocent enough boulders form horrible visions in her mind. She darts a glance at the boy and is suddenly terrified. Pericles smiles encouragement at her and then forces her gently inside. She stumbles across the earthen floor and tries desperately to push her way through the tendrils on the far side while the boy just watches her and continues his friendly smile: he has woven barbed-wire among the hanging branches and knows they are quite impenetrable.

Oh my God, thinks Tricia Hudson. 'Oh my God,' she whispers.

Pericles has not moved from the entrance. He stays there, watching.

Pericles watched the teacher take off her stockings and blow into them and move about the room singing Hark Hark the Lark gaily.

This simply cannot be, Tricia tells herself. It *can't*. Immediately she warns herself not to speak. Don't speak to him. Whatever you do, don't speak. You're sure to say the wrong thing so keep your mouth shut and don't speak.

Still the boy watches, doing nothing.

And don't panic. For God's sake don't panic, she warns herself frantically. And don't scream. Don't even move, don't bat an eye. Oh, dear God what am I to do?

Just do that for me, ma'am, said Pericles, and the beautiful lady who must be called ma'am did as she was told and said beautiful Pericles and wow Pericles and whoever taught you to do it like that?

You'll learn many wonderful things at school, Mam promised him.

Got the thievin' bastard and the little fox remained crucified for three long days and nights.

Pericles takes one step into the semi-darkness and lets the branches fall behind him: they rustle into place and lie silent. The stillness moves.

Just don't speak and don't move, Tricia Hudson warns herself again.

Then she spots the cruel polished hunting knife on the granite stone and feels certain she is about to faint.

Pericles cut Grandad up like liver, the twins chorused.

'Ma'am,' says Pericles softly, moving towards her.

Oh, God. Sweet holy God.

'Ma'am,' Pericles calls. 'I only want you to do what you were doing when I saw you through the window.'

'You're mad —' Oh, Jesus, what have I done now?

'That's all, ma'am. You looked so pretty. Really you did.' He reaches out and touches her arm gently.

Pericles reached out and touched the teacher's left mandolin and she said beautiful Pericles wherever did you learn that?

Tricia Hudson feels her body set itself rigid. She tells herself that she is about to die, denies that she is about to die, pleads with herself not to panic, warns herself to let him do anything to her as long as he does not kill her.

Pericles got his finger hooked by accident in the sky-blue nightdress and it ripped and ripped until he saw the round white belly with the little scar that someone had put there with a knife and then stuck together again. Not by accident he takes Miss Hudson's cardigan from her shoulders and hooks his finger over the top button of her blouse, pulling downwards. The cotton fabric tears readily and two perky little breasts raise their heads perkily. He sees the small pools of blood on their pinnacles and, just peeping from the top of her skirt, the scar which someone had put there with a knife and then stuck together again. But for some reason the teacher is not co-operating. She is not supposed to scream like this. Not yet, anyway. Certainly not supposed to look so frightened and pull away from him, sobbing.

Tricia Hudson screams again, a long piercing wail that takes several moments to peter out in futility.

The horned owl whooshed through the night, screaming

after edible stars, and the little fox screamed while his head was chopped off and –

'Don't scream, ma'am,' Pericles requests politely. 'I don't know why you have to scream.'

She's a proper lady and you call her ma'am.

Yes, Mam.

But somehow the lady is getting ahead of him. Or he is late again. In his labouring mind Pericles retraces his steps, running all the way. He reaches in his boot but his knife is not there. Where's that bloody knife, Dad wanted to know. Pericles is getting bewildered and for the first time in his life he is really frightened. Everything is turning upside down, and harsh hot lights flicker in his mind. The teacher is still screaming for no reason and he can't remember what he had decided to do if that happened: maybe he would remember his plan when the lightning stopped and the clock ceased its horrible clopping in his head. Now the teacher has slumped on the floor and is moaning and she looks and sounds like Vigy seducing Big Mike from her bed. She looks like Poppy in the reeds. She –

'Help me!' Tricia Hudson screams faintly.

Help, yelled Grandad and the fox and the chickens with their heads hanging off grotesquely but the fish couldn't cry: they just opened and closed their mouths silently and suffocated on the air.

'No, Ma'am,' Pericles pleads with the teacher. 'Don't scream. That's not part of it,' he explains. 'I'll tell you everything you have to do.'

Only the weakest moan escapes Miss Hudson as Pericles strips her naked and cradles her head in his arms, crooning, and stroking the back of her neck tenderly.

Bend the neck back first, Mam told him.

Pericles rocks the teacher, humming to her a song as sad and as melancholy as any Celtic dirge. He is very content now. He knows he would be happy to stay here like this for a very long time.

Bend the neck back first, Mam said again, louder.

Can't you ever do what you're told, boy, Dad shouts.

Doesn't hear unless he wants to.

Do what you're told, damn you, boy.

Bend the neck back first, Mam shouts at him.

Ah, thinks Miss Hudson, everything is going to be all right. He only wants to caress me, to love me. She sighs, her body relaxing slightly, and wonders why she had been so terrified of this gentle child.

Without thinking Pericles bends back the teacher's neck. There is a small, sharp crack, and then Miss Hudson rolls away from him, away from his arms and on to the ground: her eyes stare up at him with an odd expression of guilt and forgiveness and mild surprise.

Not dangerous, continued the doctor, unless –

Everything has gone horribly wrong. Somehow. I've got something for you ma'am. Thank you Pericles. My, you do spoil me. She isn't moving. Across the river and into the trees. But you can't have known me. Yes, ma'am. Get up, damn you.

Pericles stands up slowly and for a long time does not move, staring, utterly bewildered, at the dead teacher by his feet. She isn't supposed to be all still and quiet like this, like Grandad, like the fox. She can't be. He kneels down and cleans the pools of blood from her breasts with his tongue hoping this will help, but the dark patches remain and Tricia Hudson lies quite still and white, one leg drawn up helplessly.

Pericles remembers that he wanted to show the teacher what he had learned by watching his brother and Vigy but all that seemed pointless now. Miss Hudson refuses to do the things she did so prettily when he watched her through the window. She should be up and about, and singing and happy.

'Please get up, ma'am,' says Pericles, his voice choking. 'Please, ma'am. I've only got you.'

The teacher continues to lie perfectly still and naked and smooth at his feet.

Damn you get up, he shouted at the bloated body layed out on the parlour table, but it ignored him except to peep from under its eyelids at him.

'Please, ma'am,' Pericles pleads, crying gently. 'Just get up and everything will be fine. I promise.' He leans over and stares quizzically into the vacant eyes.

You wicked boy. Go back to your seat this instant!

Dusk falls dimly in the woods and the great horned owl deserts its hideout and wings its way like a phantom down the row of trees. Its huge eyes, swivelling incessantly, are all black pupil. It spots the solitary undefended figure of the sleeping outcast crow. Cautious, perhaps suspicious, the wise old owl circles several times, but still there is no alarm, no band of warrior crows unsheath their talons to fight him off. The lone outcast hears the sound of wings in the air as the owl checks its flight and banks, but it only stares blindly into the dark and shifts uneasily on its perch: it makes no protest as the owl drags it from the branch.

Many hours after this Pericles still keeps his watch by the teacher, touching her fondly from time to time, still mystified by what has happened. She looks very peaceful now that he has laid her out nicely, a small posy of ferns in her hands. Maybe she will retrace her steps and do everything right next time. Retrace her steps and remember him. It is only when she grows cold and unfriendly to his touch that he decides to leave her.

He walks home thoughtfully just as the sun starts to rise, filling the sky with a harsh red unfriendly light. Near the edge of the cornfield he finds a handful of soft black down. Slowly, pensively, he separates the feathers wondering at their warmth. Poor crow, he thinks, and poor little fox. Whatever happens to things when they die? He has nobody to ask about this now. Even Big Mike would not know.

Autumn

Father Denis Redmond, his hands clasped tightly behind his head, fingers interlaced, in an effort to prevent them shaking (a fruitless exercise as it turns out) stares sadly out of the window that looks on to the garden from his study. All things seem to be preparing for death. The trees have long since started to bare themselves of foliage, and he has noticed the eyes of old people turn inwards and has heard them pray more rapidly as though fearful they would be cut off before completing their self-imposed quota of supplications to their preferred saints. It is the time of year, he reflects morbidly, when he must inspect the black-and-silver requiem vestments for signs of mothly feasting, time, also, to brace himself against the cloying sweet stench of lilies. Moving his head slightly he catches sight of his reflection in the window and, shuddering involuntarily, contemplates death staring him in the face. Not a pretty sight by any standards. Far away, beyond what now appears to have become his own gloomy death mask, beyond the neglected herbaceous border, beyond the cornfields with their few remaining uncollected but hoodered stacks, he witnesses the re-enactment of that extraordinary drama performed in the kitchen of the small farmhouse, only now it takes on a somewhat different aspect.

I *knew* it would come to something like this, the man said, white-faced with anger.

His wife cowered from him, her lips drawn tight, so tight they were almost bloodless.

Naked. Bloody naked. Not a damn stitch left on her, and exposing herself to everyone, the man went on, bewildered perhaps by his own inability to comprehend or cope with this appalling situation.

Oh sweet Jesus, his wife suddenly wailed, breaking down, sobbing, her eyes pleading with Father Redmond.

And her neck cracked –

Don't, Bill –

cracked to bits, the man exaggerated.

His wife sobbed louder, holding herself and rocking like a woman in unbearable physical pain.

And it's all your fault. Always protecting him and saying he was just a child –

The woman had no answer for this.

Well, her husband shouted, that's all done with now.

Ohhh, the woman wailed.

Suddenly the man rounded on Father Redmond who had inoffensively been trying to cope with some appalling situation of his own. I told her right from the start that the boy was mad, father, but she insisted that he was all right, especially after you – He swung back to his wife: Are you going to tell me where you've hidden him?

Mam (as a small grubby child called her nervously from the door) did not look at anyone directly. Her face was squeezed of emotion and there remained only a confused petulance. Her thin mouth was dry and scored by many tiny vertical cracks, her skin had taken on the sheen of wax overnight. It seemed for a moment as though she was about to speak but changed her mind. She shook her head (an action which did not appear negative, did not, indeed, appear to have any connection with the man's question), weeping steadily.

I'm talking to you, damn it, the man shouted. Where the hell is he?

Mam let the tears stream down her face unheeded, and rocked herself desolately back and forth in the wooden chair, hugging herself tighter in silent anguish.

The man turned again to Father Redmond. I've got to find

him for his own sake, he explained and lowered his voice as though what he was about to add demanded secrecy. The people in the village are out for blood. They'll tear the fool to pieces if I don't find him first.

Father Redmond coughed: Don't you think you should call Sergeant Bullock?

You think I didn't? He's no damn use. Farting about and calling reinforcements from the mainland.

Well, said Father Redmond, always happy to postpone the inevitable, don't you think you should wait until they –

Wait? How can I wait, father? Christ alone knows what might happen if I don't find that boy. He could kill someone else.

Hell, Mam, a red-haired young man called Big Mike put in, Dad's only trying to help him. There's no use thinking we can cover this one up.

He's right, woman. If you won't listen to me then listen to Mike, the man said, his voice kinder.

Can't you wait for Patrick to get the other policemen and let them find him? Mam pleaded. (I'll wait for you, Eileen, Patrick Bullock lied and I'll wait for you, Patrick, Eileen Ferris lied back.)

Jesus God, woman, you just don't understand, do you? The men are so frightened at what he might do next they're ready to go out and find him and kill him if I don't find the boy first.

Oh, no, Mam wailed.

Oh, yes, Dad told her. Please, please, woman, tell me where he is.

I don't know, Mam screamed suddenly and the shrillness of her voice made them all jump. Then, in a whisper: I just don't know where he is, Bill. I'd tell you if I did.

You must have *some* idea, Mam, Big Mike coaxed.

Mam shook her head.

Think, woman, Dad urged.

I have thought, Mam said. I'm tired of thinking. I just don't know where he is. Then she choked and went back to weeping silently.

Father Denis Redmond turns from the window and sets out with grim determination for the cupboard in the corner of the room while the meagre pageant still unfolds and accompanies him across the worn carpet. Might it be that it had another meaning, had all taken place at some other time and on another stage, for it seemed now possessed of an odd unintentional humour? He sees these people playing out their tragedy like spirits appearing to grow weightless, their hard leathery faces growing harder the closer they hover about him; those fiercely proud peasant faces resembling cheerful enough demons, attempting, tongue in cheek, to cajole him into some Chaucerian kankedort from which he would undoubtedly escape, becoming more and more like familiars he had hurt and betrayed through the years. And perhaps all this wasn't so very ludicrous. For while he had striven from student to sub-deacon and from deacon to priest had not the face of life *seemed* clear enough but had it not, too, been masked, friends and enemies – real and imagined – ever less identifiable? And had it not come to pass that the more zealous he became the more life tended to dissemble, to become what it undoubtedly was now: a perpetual and ghastly epiphany caricaturing his sunken dreams?

Father Redmond stares in wonderment (which in no way diminishes his gratitude) at the well-filled crystal tumbler that has so miraculously appeared in his twitching hand. Ah, but had he only believed in God and willed His friendship the very spirituality of His nature might have been an ally and indicated the wise and holy way. Then there would have been no spiralling downwards through unreal voices; there could have been the infinite uplifting, the divine evolution in which his own spirit and Christ's joined and became entire and perfect. And yet . . . and yet . . . Father Redmond sinks into the ravaged chair and sighs heavily. A light, firm wind sighs even more heavily across the garden and makes the gate rattle with the unmusical metallic clatter of a cracked bell. Soothed by the drink so providentially served by the benevolent spirit who for the moment wishes to remain anonymous, he lies back in the chair and watches darkness roll in on soundless padded feet, night's stealthy bailiff surreptitiously invading his room and making even his most familiar possessions fade into obscurity before his very eyes. How very like dying it must be, and how rapidly it overtakes one! Yet not as rapidly, it seems, as the sudden unwelcome memory of his frantic anguished letter to the bishop which neither of them had ever mentioned:

– and that is how you see me stand, Matthew: straddling the gaping chasm which divides knowledge and faith, the shunting echoes of hope and mercy weaving dreadful visions of what *is* and concealing (but not completely for that would make repentance too facile) what might have been. Sometimes I feel myself possessed of a diabolic urge to destroy myself before I can destroy God's love. What presumption! you might say, and you would probably be justified. Yet the faith I know I once had – and surely, Matthew, you can recall that time or was it really so very long ago? – was tinged with a bewildering jealousy as if, even then, I was haunted by the premonition that it was only on loan and would be withdrawn from me in time. Oh, Matthew, do not ever let them fool you into believing that time heals. That is an outrageous lie. You cannot expect to know God, I seem to hear a voice saying. Yet sometimes, when I consecrate the Host (but more often, alas, when I hide my soul in shadows and die my own pathetic death) I do know Him. And I hear Him if only as a tiny roar, a melancholy roar out of reach yet within reach, receding or moving towards me, but always on hand to save me. Then the moment is gone and He has done nothing . . .

Oh, Matthew, I am dying without Him . . .

And now at last, although the feeling has been haunting him for considerably longer than he would care to admit, he knows the cruel irrevocable impact of the knowledge which only animals seem able to recognize, and accept with equanimity, that one will soon be dead – that, indeed, one has already removed one's shroud from the locker, brushed it, and has placed one arm in a sleeve. I can no longer postpone death. I can no longer employ quixotic tactics to delay the one real inevitability by as much as a few hours. On the other hand: I have *some* time left in hand, which is a good thing. I can *still* make amends. I still have some hope of – You really are incredible, says the wind in a sudden gust of frustrated anger. You have no time whatsoever left, rattles the gate rustily. And you are no earthly use to anyone, spits the fire; which meant he had lit it himself without burning the house down which was encouraging. Father Redmond tries desperately to gather his thoughts.

I sometimes wish the Church would allow us to believe in the concept of reincarnation, the Bishop had said or was saying.

An odd sort of thing for a theologian of your standing to wish, Matthew. You are not, I trust, about to start another schism?

Ha. No, no. I was just thinking it would make it a lot easier for me to understand you.

Me? Really? Pray go on –

I would have thought you were undoubtedly someone like Ryder in your last terrestrial junket.

Ryder? Who in the name of all that is holy is –

Albert Pinkham Ryder, that somewhat eccentric painter. American of course. You haven't heard of him?

Not a whisper!

I am surprised. I would have thought that you and he would be well acquainted.

Not even on nodding terms, I'm afraid.

Hmmm. The bishop's head nodded solemnly.

I wish you'd explain, Matthew. I worry about these episcopal ravings.

He never completed anything, the Bishop replied. Did and

redid every canvas until they were so thickly textured with candlewax and varnish and oil and alcohol –

Ah! I'm beginning to get the –

No, that's not the similarity I was referring to. They collapsed under the weight of his inordinate desire for absolute perfection, the Bishop said. If you get my point.

I'm afraid I don't, apart from the obvious. I wish you'd clarify –

But the Bishop wouldn't, had, in fact, nothing more to say for the moment. Christ! Father Redmond, in an effort to rid himself of the prelate's unnecessary interference, takes another drink. It is useless to battle further with these thoughts, better to surrender honourably and let them have their own way. At least they are a little less morbid than those which preceded them; although he realizes he will be back on that tack soon enough if he doesn't watch out.

Father Redmond finds himself once more face to face with his downcast reflection in the window. And like that reflection, he ponders mournfully, the truth has got to be faced at last: down he had fallen, downhill all the way – still, something consoled him, it was not yet quite the bottom. It was as if his hectic slide had terminated in a gigantic gaping abyss yawning below him, over which he had started to fly; but the chances of him clearing it were exceedingly slim. And yet, even now, all hope was not lost: somewhere within himself he had the power to land securely on the opposite side. It seemed that there was one particular act which would certainly bring matters to a satisfactory conclusion. And as he hung suspended midway between safety and disaster he was surrounded by men whose faces he vaguely recognized, who spoke as though he was not there, who directed their words at a round-shouldered, tired little man who looked as bewildered as himself:

Come on, Bill, you'll have to tell us sooner or later where the boy is. We don't want to harm him.

He's bloody dangerous loose like that, Bill.

We understand you've got to put on some show of protecting him for the wife's sake but –

We'll keep the dogs on their leads while they sniff him out and then we'll hold him 'till Bullock –

– wish you'd tell us before he does any more to harm himself.

Father Redmond shuts his eyes hard for a moment and then lets them open slowly, hopefully: alas, he is still where he was, perhaps has already crashed to the bottom of the ravine.

Denis is going to be a priest! Father Redmond could hear his mother's voice as clear as the flute she frequently played in the Rathmines Ladies Ensemble. Oddly enough she had been in no way surprised. She had accepted his decision with the same defiant calm she accepted everything she could not quite fathom: she called these phenomena 'the will of God' and was pleased to place responsibility for their orchestration firmly in the lap of the Almighty. She had even managed, she told Mrs Frogley, violinist, and Mrs Hamilton, cellist – slighting Mrs Loftus, pianist, who was in her bad books, and given to arriving late for rehearsals and biting her nails – to read signs of his impending vocation into his various activities between leaving school and his decision to enter the seminary; and this took some doing. For Denis Redmond, boy soprano of note, actor, steward, creator of verse (*not* poetry), linguist extraordinary, con-man (if only of himself) and, for nine hectic days, second trumpet in the Mentwich Colliery Brass Band had at no time given public indication of a spiritual bent. Of all his activities only the acting had continued to play any significant part in his life, and certainly he had as much reason as any to be grateful for that talent. But Denis Redmond, if he had not quite reached the limelit heights of Roddy McDowell or Freddy Bartholomew, could always boast he had once enjoyed the reputation of a potentially tremendous talent. Unlike so much about him now there was nothing spurious about this reputation, the pinnacle of his short-lived career being a quite extraordinarily precocious portrayal of the beleaguered naval cadet in The

Winslow Boy. The Birth of a New Dramatic Star, the pundits hailed his debut, and he was even labelled 'the thrilling magician of emotions' – whatever that was supposed to mean. The play opened originally for a run of two weeks, but was forced to stay for four months by public demand. Denis Redmond youthfully basked in the adulation, and thoroughly enjoyed acting – and it was to strike him from time to time in the years that followed that he had been play-acting ever since.

Father Redmond smiles ruefully at the ruefully smiling face which shifts position uneasily in the window. Dear God, how very long ago it all seemed! Two lifetimes ago. More. But not quite as long ago, it appeared absurdly, as the day he was ordained a priest of the Holy Roman and Apostolic Church, that fantastic day, miraculous day when the Archbishop anointed his hands and bound them, and he felt himself washed by the tremendous love of Christ; a day somewhat sullied by the grotesque theatrics of the evening editions of the city's newspapers which took up his story with trivial relish, describing it with banner headlines such as CHILD STAR ORDAINED, RONNIE NOW REVEREND and, most inanely but prophetically, WINSLOW BOY FACES NEW TRIAL, and all as though the intervening years had counted for nothing. Perhaps they were right. Perhaps they knew something he didn't, but they could hardly have been aware of the hand of God perpetually on his shoulder nor of the tempestuous battles which raged in his conscience as he struggled to justify what ultimately emerged as his only possible vocation. Nor could they have known the fierce doubts and depressions that stalked his every ejaculation as he prayerfully proclaimed his unworthiness, the hopeless emptiness he suffered despite achieving his doctorate in both philosophy and theology, no small honour, and developing into something of an international expert (and often consulted as such) in Church History. It may very well have been his incisive intellectual alertness which caused his most grievous misgivings since they transformed the simple face of faith into something of a metaphysical nightmare and made prayer appear a wilfully redundant form of transpiritual communication, and while this was all perhaps a matter of opinion it was also something for which he never wholly forgave God.

On the other hand his fellow seminarians (mainly from working-class or farming backgrounds with no great aspirations other than practical day to day ministry, and considerably younger than himself) differed very little from the boisterous adolescents he had knocked about with at school and were, by and large, as decent and normal a collection of young men as one could wish to meet. And why shouldn't they be? Still, anyone worth his Catholic salt knew that the 'call' carried with it the burden of solemnity, did it not? But this particular squad in no way laboured under such archaic misconceptions; they were, it seemed, on delightfully amicable terms with God and not above sharing their private jokes with Him. But Denis Redmond, possibly because he demanded too much sanctity of himself, found little about which to be light-hearted or joyous. He plummeted deeper into despair and at one point, after a particularly horrific visitation from the spectre of his own unworthiness, even thought of quitting the seminary and quietly vanishing from the face of the earth. As for God, Denis Redmond's theology professor had said to him with a truly remarkable ecclesiastical acceptance: You know, Denis, you must never expect to *know* God. What would be the point of faith if you did? And he was right, of course. Yet Denis Redmond felt trapped: the more completely for the realization that in no way could he escape the commitment he had made. Of his vocation he was certain, of Christ – well. Of Christ he was certain in a doubtful way, but he was young enough then to hope he would find Him.

Alas, I have not, Father Redmond thinks, noting his hands are inauspiciously empty and demanding to be clasped together once more. At least not the loving, saving Christ I had hoped for, although He often seemed to be playing a carefree game of hide-and-seek and often, too, seemed on the verge of discovery. From the back of his mind Father Redmond hears the hard rasping voice again: we'll keep the dogs on their leads and just get them to sniff him out.

Pericles heard this also and his body stiffened. He knew the dogs well: lurchers and Staffordshires used for badger hunting, vicious brutes starved and beaten into total hatred but wonderful hunters for all that. He had a great respect for their power of destruction. He slid from his hiding place among the rafters and crept silently from the house.

Like a bloody animal, he is, Dad said, the way he creeps about and hides himself.

Pericles knows he can conceal himself very well, merging into shadows with incredible ease. He can sit motionless for hours in the most unlikely positions. Sometimes he has what Mam calls his fits and this helps, but mostly he can manage without whatever fits are, as he is doing now, listening.

'What are you going to do if you do find him, Dad?' Big Mike who usually knows everything would like to know.

Dad shakes his head: 'Kindest thing I could do would be shoot him,' he says with strange tenderness. 'But I suppose they'd hang me for that.'

'Surely would,' agrees Big Mike readily.

'Can't just leave him running wild,' Dad continues. 'Can't wait for bloody Bullock to get off his arse. And I don't trust that lot,' he adds jerking his thumb in the direction of the village. 'I've seen them lusting for blood once they start hunting.'

'Jesus, they'd never let the dogs loose after him, would they?' Big Mike asks, horrified.

'You never know with that lot when their blood is up,' Dad says. 'After all . . .' He seems to forget what he is about to say, his words waylaid by private thoughts.

Pericles thinks he hears someone suggest: we could exorcise him, I suppose: but then he remembers that he has heard this at some other time and recalls how foolish he felt on his knees until someone thought to tell him to get up.

'Poor Mam's in an awful state,' Big Mike points out. 'I've never seen her this bad. She'll die if anything happens to him,' he added, shaking his head, confused, even bitter, as though Mam, usually so solid, so strong, so capable had no right to emotions of this nature. 'Maybe we could – '

'Something has got to happen to him and your mother better make up her mind to that: he'll have to be locked up in one of those asylums at the very least,' Dad says. 'Maybe we could what?'

'Oh. Maybe, I was thinking, maybe when we find him we could ship him off somewhere,' suggests Big Mike vaguely, blushing as though only now realizing the stupidity of the suggestion.

'Where?' Dad asks quickly, snatching at the possibility, his mind predatory and willing to chase any feeble thought. But then: 'How could we do that, Mike? Where could we send him without everyone asking questions? It's too late for that anyway now that Bullock's been told.' 'I dunno,' falters Big Mike, amazed that his father was even considering the possibility. 'Australia, maybe. They used to ship – '

'Don't be daft, boy. How could he cope in Australia by himself?'

'It was just an idea.'

'Huh.'

'Well, have you decided what you're going to do?'

Dad shakes his head forlornly.

'You'll have to make up your mind soon, Dad, and do *something*,' Big Mike urges. 'You'll never forgive yourself if you do nothing and – '

'I'm trying to think,' Dad snaps. He paces about the kitchen, lifting things and putting them down again, glancing at the pictures and calendars as though they might have an answer. 'There must be something we can do,' he adds, his voice showing that he doesn't really believe there is.

'Like what?'

'That's what I'm trying to think, you ape,' Dad says.

'How about – nothing.' Big Mike decides against any more suggestions at the sight of Dad's ferocious glare.

'Oh God,' moans Dad, 'what have we landed ourselves in?'

Pericles is puzzled by the conversation and tries to figure it out from his new hiding place inside the empty water-barrel by the side of the house under the kitchen window. He sucks quietly on the marrow of a bone filched from the scraps left out for the dog the night before: the hound, perhaps sensitive to impending tragedy, made no protest. The solitary crow made no protest as the horned owl swept into the night. Got the thievin' bastard, someone shouted, and hurled the decapitated little fox on the woodpile. Everything has gone wrong. He must retrace his steps and start from the very beginning again, ma'am.

'Oh, don't let the dogs at him,' Mam wails from her chair. 'Wait for Sergeant Bullock to come with his men from the mainland,' she pleads. She has become the image of Grandma who does not leave her room anymore but prepares secretly to die. Mind his head.

'Wait for the police,' Mam begs again. 'The men can be so cruel. They'll kill him, I know. And he not even knowing what he was doing, I'm sure.'

'Nobody's going to kill him, woman,' Dad assures her, but some instinct tells him he may very well have to in the end.

'He's just not right in the head,' Mam adds fatuously.

'Huh,' grunts Dad but not unkindly.

Pericles smiles and gazes far back in his mind. The nicely dressed gentlemen and the lovely ladies astride their well-groomed shining horses gallop after the plump little red fox. The lean strong hounds bay balefully and lead the ladies and gentlemen atop their sweating horses a merry chase after the exhausted panting fox. Wherever had he seen this?

'Well,' announces Dad, straightening his back and smoothing his hair in an odd gesture of determination, 'we'll have to try and find him before they get back with those damn dogs.'

Pericles stops smiling.

'Oh, you have to stop them, Bill. You wouldn't let them use the dogs to find him – '

Dad looks away quickly.

Pericles stood on top of the wall surrounding the cornfield and watched the workmen scoading laboriously, steam rising from the stinking load in the cart and across his vision the fox raced ahead of the yowling hounds, panting. The jailed bird thumped its little heart ten times and the teacher panted as she made the moon rise in the top left hand corner of the blackboard. And this is, she said defiantly. Oh my God, no. The fox chewed the neat little pile of bones and disappeared into the evening as Pericles had tried to disappear into every evening. Hounds still bayed and loped after the fox in ever decreasing circles. She smelled of babysoap even on weekdays. The fox held its breath and slipped, quiet as a snake, away from the pursuers. Got the thievin' bastard.

Pericles hears the yelping dogs long before the Ford pickup rattles into the yard. Nat Dawson jumps out, officiously giving the peak of his cap a smart tug. Pericles sees that all the men are dressed for hunting. The dogs strain at their leashes and yelp abuse at their handlers.

'Well, Bill,' Nat Dawson says in the gruff embarrassed voice of a man who has reached, reluctantly, the point of no return, 'are you still going to make us go and look for him?'

'I've told you, Nat. I just don't know where he is,' Dad says, sounding very tired.

'Don't let the dogs get him,' Mam begs quietly of the old range.

'I believe you,' Nat Watson tells Dad. 'But –

'I'm going to wait for Bullock and his men to come,' Dad says, glancing at Mam. 'If you go after him with that lot you could frighten him into doing something – '

'It's to stop him doing something more that we want to find him,' Nat Watson points out reasonably enough. 'You'd think we were enjoying this, Bill.'

Dad stares at him hard.

'Why don't you come with us and you can see that nothing happens?' Dad shakes his head. 'I'll stay with the woman,' he says. 'She's in a bad way. Besides, I want no part of – '

Nat Hudson sighs. 'I'm sorry, Bill. The men have decided it isn't safe to leave the lad roaming about on his own. Who'd be next?'

Dad's eyes are fixed on the dogs.

'Damn you, what's the matter with you bastards,' shouts Phillip Busby, and tugs viciously at the two brindle Staffordshires which strain towards the side of the house.

Git, said Grandma, and the hound left the kitchen on its belly.

Pericles knows that the dogs have spotted him with their noses and that it won't be long before their persistence drags the man to his hiding place. He eases himself out of the barrel and slips around the back of the house, dashes across the small vegetable plot, and vaults the low stone wall like a shadow. Across the field he races, his feet sinking deeply into the earth now that the field has been ploughed. He runs as fast as he can until he reaches the lane to the school and then stops abruptly. The land is deserted and very quiet, the only sound coming from the woods to his left: the rhythmic crack of someone axing a tree. Behind him the dogs swing within range of his hearing, yodelling sonorously as they seek his scent with their wide nostrils.

'Don't let them go,' Mam pleads. 'Please, Bill, I'm begging you, don't let them go.'

I have to go, Patrick Bullock told Eileen Ferris. There's nothing for me here but you.

I know, Patrick.

I'll come back for you, Eileen.

Shhhsh.

And then: I've come back, Eileen. You haven't changed.

Too late, Patrick. Too late.

And you with a houseful of children.

Yes.

And the strange one.

Strange?

So I've heard tell.

Oh, no. He's my beautiful boy, my lovely boy.

– ?

He's so dear to me, Patrick. All the while I've told myself he was ours. Yours and mine.

But –

I know he isn't. Not even my own. But don't you understand? He kept you close to me.

'I can't stop them now,' Dad says, and sits opposite her, wondering what is to become of them all.

Each time I touched him I touched you, Patrick. You see you have been with me all the years.

Ah.

All the love I kept stored up within me for you I gave to him and he seemed to understand. That was the lovely thing, Patrick. My lovely boy seemed to understand.

'Where the fuck is Bullock?' Dad demands loudly, lurching to his feet and thumping the table in frustration.

'He'll be back,' Mam says quietly, wistfully.

'Back?'

'Oh yes,' Mam says. 'He promised.'

Dad takes Big Mike by the arm and led him to the door. 'You go after them, Mike, and watch out for the boy. I'll wait for Bullock.'

'What's got into Mam?' Big Mike asks bewildered.

Dad shakes his head again. 'I don't know. I just don't know. I'd be afraid to leave her alone now, though.'

Father Redmond frees himself from the rampant wallydrags with a vigorous shake of his body. Almost for succour he gazes out at the deepening darkness. Far out across the rolling farmland great activity seems to be taking place. He can just make out the flicker of lighted torches and there seems to be the desolate sound of dogs howling. Then a man shouts, his voice a disembodied echo calling back hollowly in the night, and the dogs raise their chant a semitone. The lights congregate in a tight circle, and then fan out again.

What I would like to know, Father Redmond informed the bishop who was certainly showing near beatific patience, what I would really like to know is what lunatic – I've forgotten what I was going to say – . . .

– no I haven't! Shall I start again?

It would help, certainly –

Right. What I would really like to know is what delirium tremensic ass called it bringing light to the world?

I think he meant – whoever he was – to enlighten –

– when one's own soul is a soulless petrified residue of extinct doctrine –

Come now, Denis –

– in which even the loneliest faith refuses to be comforted.

Perhaps there is no time for comfort –

Whyever not, Matthew? Father Redmond asked urgently, sensing that the bishop, like God had been on the odd occasion, was on the point of saying something important.

– since, the bishop was saying if not so importantly but with a kindly look of jocose seriousness in his eye all the same, all its waking hours are wholly occupied in a vain effort to rescue itself from drowning.

Ah! Very devious, my lord bishop. But as you will have noticed I have had nothing to drink for well over an hour. Father Redmond raised a hopeful eyebrow.

I can offer you a cup of tea –

I think not. I'm allergic to tannin –

You really are no better, are you, Denis?

Indeed I am. A new man as the saying goes, insisted Father Redmond straightening his shoulders and rotating his arms wildly above his head in an extravagant display of physical fitness.

Alas, the bishop remained unimpressed by this exhibition of well-being it seemed: You do realize that your suspension is only a matter of time?

Good God why? I've –

Oh, do stop play-acting, Denis. Please. The stories fly in every day about your monstrous behaviour. My desk is littered with letters of complaint. I agree they are probably grossly exaggerated but you simply cannot go on –

How true –

Now stop it! Stop this morbid self-pity once and for all. You make me so angry –

I'm sorry, Matthew. I have tried.

I know you have, the bishop sighed compassionately. That's precisely why I've given you so many chances. Good heavens, Denis, do you really think I would have tolerated your stupidity as long as I have if I didn't believe you were trying? By the way, I don't suppose there *is* any truth in these black masses – ?

Black masses? Good Lord –

And exorcisms?

Oh, that –

Father Redmond raises both eyebrows in an effort to see more clearly what all these flickering lights can mean but with little success for it is as though his eyelids have been shredded and are fluttering about him, punctuating the guilty chatterings of his mind.

Pericles can see the lights clearly: they look strangely pretty. Miss Hudson added stars and planets at random on the blackboard scene but they didn't twinkle. Toc. Toc. Pericles tapped the window with his nail. Toc. The fox's life continued to fall from the woodpile.

Pericles stands expressionless in the centre of the lane, his mind wrenched. If the teacher is lying quietly under the willow he should be there with her, should he not. It is so unkind to leave her there alone, her ten toes unmoving, one leg drawn up, her hand half-raised in astounded salutation. He starts to run again, brushing aside the night-nits which hum aggressively about him. But he runs economically, spacing his strides. The hounds bay balefully after the little fox. Got the thievin' bastard. Like some bloody animal he is. Oh, my lovely boy. Pericles hears the shouts of the hunters as they urge the dogs to find the scent, and he runs steadily down the lane.

'Hang on to those leads, lads,' a voice bellows, 'or they'll have him in shreds now their blood is up.'

The excited dogs howl nearer while the little fox slithers into the night and vanishes and Pericles changes direction, turning off the lane. He decides to make for the shelter of the woods that welcome him so gladly, and sets off across the open field, running faster now. When he gets tired he will vanish into the night, he tells himself: is, in fact, already disappearing. That will fool them. A strange exhilaration comes over him as he watches himself vanish into the darkness like the poor little fox.

'Get those fucking dogs back, for Christ's sake!' someone roars frantically behind him. It sounds a lot like Big Mike.

Pericles bent down and patted Biddy Ferguson's bitch that was expecting her pups any day soon and laid out the food in neat piles beside the teacher. Why thank you, Pericles, you really mustn't spoil me. But tell me, is it far from here? Oh no, ma'am, it isn't, and Pericles knows it can't be since the dogs are getting much closer now and there seems to be so little time left.

'You try getting them back, Mike,' the answer comes. 'You know damn well they'll turn on us if we try and stop them now.'

'Jesus!' The screamed ejaculation is heard even above the din of the dogs.

'Get back here, fuck you! Christ, I'm being taken off my feet.'

'Oh, Jesus!'

From his window Father Denis Redmond watches the boy racing diagonally across the field. He sees the lights break clear of the boundary hedge one by one until they form a ghostly shining semi-circle in the field. At first he cannot understand what is taking place, but suddenly a familiar sense of imminent horror overcomes him. Only this time there is more to it: that small forlorn bent figure so closely pursued by the burning sinister lights is himself. Through his jittering lashes, through that special howling limbo which lonely dying men can recognize, he watches himself stumble, fall on one knee, and then, with a heaving frightened sob, race on again. Dear Jesus, he thinks bewildered, this is a dreadful way to die. But not for the moment, it appears, since help is at hand; help in the shape of himself running from yet another direction, running with a speed that would have astounded him had he thought about it, speed accelerated by some mysterious knowledge which hinted that at the end of this particular race some form of absolution would surely be waiting.

But what is certain, he realizes, if only because of the painful heaving in his chest as he sucks the cold evening mist into his lungs, is that he is running as he has never before run in his life, undeterred by the comical sight he must be, naked, as he is, apart from a pair of red silk Sinbadian carpet slippers with long curled toes like the prow of a gondola, arms outstretched to the panting frightened figure a hundred yards away.

'The leads have snapped,' a voice yells.

'Jesus Christ!' another voice swears. And then: 'Christ – who's that mad bugger?'

'God above – it's the priest!'

'Get back, father!'

'Stop him, will you!'

'They've got the boy – '

Oh, Jesus – '

Dad held him by the neck and whipped him cruelly. Pericles feels the sting of the whip and enjoys not letting his father see that it hurts. He feels it cut into his leg and the little fox screams out and blood drips on to its clotted brush and only stops when he is stretched out in the sun. Again he feels Dad's lash bite into his leg, his calves, his thighs and he grits his teeth and keeps smiling.

'Pull those fucking dogs off!'

'Keep away, father!'

'Get him back, will you?'

Be quiet! snapped Miss Hudson.

'Be quiet!' screams Pericles, but the dogs ignore him and continue to rip long slivers of warm flesh from the tired little fox.

'Christ Almighty! They're going to kill him.'

'They're eating him alive. Oh my God. My *God*!'

Pericles shudders violently as Dad's whip cuts remorselessly into his back, his chest, his face. Suddenly the sharp tongue of twisted leather catches his throat and flicks it neatly away from him. Got the thievin' bastard, someone whispers to him triumphantly.

Beautiful Pericles, whispers Miss Hudson.

We'll get on famously now.

The owl whooshed through the night, its talons extended, and carried him off.

Father Redmond launches himself wildly at the dogs, trying to cover the boy's torn and bleeding body with his own. At first he feels a queer pride, a sense of generosity, of nobility almost, of which he had long since thought himself incapable. Then, with detached calm, he realizes that the animals have not backed off as he had anticipated they would, but are now attacking his own body with renewed daemonic savagery. Strange, he thinks, that I can feel no pain, only what seems to be a soft and cooling rain.

Shadows cluster over him, pulling at his arms, trying to help him to his feet, perhaps even trying to sober him, or offer him a drink. He feels life start to shiver from him with extraordinary precision, dripping slowly and methodically from his veins into the tattered quiet body beneath him. A compassionate face, square and red but gentle nevertheless, emerges from the mist gathering about his vision.

'Father,' it begins, but if it said any more it is lost, devoured by the frenzied hostile snarling. Staccato words are lobbed singly yet in an odd way linked into his mind.

– back – we're – law.

– oh – lovely – boy.

– tried – not – hold.

Stand back.

Another face, not unlike the first but surmounted by an official-looking cap with a shiny peak, peers at him. 'I am the police, father,' it announces. 'You'll be all right now, father,' – which was nice to know.

Now he is walking in a beautiful garden through which a small perfumed river flows, a garden planted with the most incredible coloured flowers which preen themselves in a gentle caressing breeze filled with the strains of music – de Falla, perhaps, or Respighi. He is alone. Where is everybody? Ah, not quite alone it seems. Infinitely forlorn tableaux appear and dissolve before him: Oscar Wilde, handcuffed, head bowed, mocked, spat at, stands weeping on the desolate platform of Clapham Junction; Rudolf Guglielmo poses uncomfortably for a photograph in rented clothes, fades, re-emerges as Valentino and tries to con him into buying a bottle of Mineral-ava; Gandhi stares incredulously at his killer wondering what he has done to deserve such an end even as he collapses in the dust; a petrified little Florence Sass cowers beneath her Turkish slave-driver waiting for her beloved Sam to rescue her with a bid of five pounds; Raoul Wallenberg's generous face, now ghastly and pallid, peers through the bars of some remote

Soviet prison and cries Save me, save me. Immediately the word 'salvation' takes complete possession of Father Redmond's mind. Salvation! The promised reward for all those sacrifices he had promised to make. Only it had not quite worked out that way. Still, for the moment, it seems as though he might be on the point of salvation. Confused ideals out of which his downfall has grown reveal themselves clearly: only now it is too late, too late by far to do anything about it. Yet someone had called him 'father' which was comfort indeed to his soul even if, at the same time, something warns him not to try and read too much into that, and to watch his step. Watch the step, says his friend the bishop and with this fatherly advice is gone. No other kindly samaritan seems to be forthcoming as he feels life ebb from him. Or is there. 'Thank you, father,' a sobbing woman's voice is saying away in the distance. 'Thank you for trying to save my lovely boy.' And yet more: it is so perplexing but there is still the sound of many voices about him, voices which should have receded by now, voices which seem genuinely anxious and concerned, which seem willing to make allowances for his stupidity, for all his shortcomings. How could he have felt so wretchedly abandoned when these hovering shadows above him beg for nothing less than forgiveness? Forgive us, father, they are certainly crying, a touching majesty in their contrition, and he repeats the words aloud himself: forgive me father. But it does nothing to set his mind at rest. Suddenly, with a crazed and terrifying energy that came from nowhere, he screams: Forgive me Father! And it is as though this agonized plea is just a whisper, and is whisked away from him, is about to be accepted. Alas, almost in the twinkling of an eye it is tossed back at him, is rejected. Each shape above him crowds closer, huddling together as if for mutual protection against some uncertain wrath, leaning over him, touching him, watching, whispering, sobbing, mourning. Oh, Patrick, Patrick you came too late, a sad dehumanized voice seems to whisper. He wants to explain he is not Patrick. He wants quiet. He wants peace. He wants – you can hardly expect to *know* God, someone tells him. It is too late anyway, the bailiffs are coming. You are wasting your time. You are so utterly useless, another voice tells him – and with that everyone has vanished.

Out of pity and with an odd reverence one of the men throws an old sack stained with badger blood over his lifeless, naked body.